IRISH FAIRYTALES

MICHAEL SCOTT

ILLUSTRATED BY
JOSEPH GERVIN

MERCIER PRESS

Mercier Press
PO Box 5, 5 French Church Street, Cork
24 Lower Abbey Street, Dublin 1

Text © Michael Scott, 1988
Illustrations © Joseph Gervin, 1988

First published by Sphere Books Limited in 1985 under the title
Tales from the Land of Erin, Volume 1. This edition first published in
1988.

A CIP record for this book is available from the British Library.

ISBN 0 85342 866 2

10 9 8 7 6 5 4 3

FOR COURTNEY: A FIRST EDITION

Printed in Ireland by Colour Books Ltd.

Contents

1. The Arrival of the Tuatha de Danann in Erin:
   The Stowaway   *page* 7
2. The Departure of the Tuatha de Danann:
   The Secret Places   28
3. The Fairy Horses   33
4. The King's Secret   48
5. The Crow Goddess   56
6. The Fairies' Revenge   62
7. The Fairy Dance   71
8. The Wise Woman's Payment   81
9. The Shoemaker and Himself   90
10. The Fairy Harper   109
11. The Floating Island   117

The Arrival Of The Tuatha De Danann In Erin: The Stowaway

The land of Erin was invaded many times in the past, and amongst the greatest of its invaders were the Tuatha De Danann, who were called the People of the Goddess. They were powerful magicians and they brought to the island many, many gifts, including the arts of healing, writing and metal-working.

However, how they discovered Erin is a strange tale, for they found it almost by accident. . .

The ship was made of solid gold.

Daire stood on the dockside and stared up at the beautiful vessel. It was twice as long as any ship he had ever seen before – long and slender, high at both ends and with a sail that shimmered in the early morning sun like silk. It was a truly magical craft.

All the inhabitants of the city of Murias were talking about the ship – which was to be called the *Seeker* – and the voyage it was preparing to make. There were rumours that the four tribes of the Tuatha De Danann would soon be sailing to a new land. But the *Seeker* would go first and find that new land for the People of the Goddess.

Of course, everyone wanted to be on that ship, but only the best had been chosen. They had come from the four magical cities of Finias, Gorias, Falias and from Murias itself. The bravest warriors, the finest magicians, sorcerers and physicians, the best carpenters and metal-workers would be going. Even the king and his court would be sailing on the *Seeker*. Once a suitable land had been found, they would set

-the seeker-

about making it ready for the rest of their race.

Daire had been standing on the dock since sunrise. He was a young boy of about ten years old, with a mop of thick black hair and sharp black-coloured eyes in a thin, almost pointed face. He had stood watching the men come and go, the food and weapons being loaded and the famous people who would sometimes appear on deck. He had even seen Diancecht, the doctor and magician who had discovered the art of healing and curing. He had arrived in his carriage of polished black metal, which was drawn by two snow-white unicorns.

The young boy stood back as a troop of soldiers in their silver armour marched down to the dock and up the ramp to the ship. They wore the crest of the Black Crow, the sign of Morrigan, one of the great women warriors of the De Danann people.

Oh, how he wished he were going. But he was only the son of a blacksmith, although his father always claimed that

the family were related to Goibniu, the famous blacksmith, who had actually discovered how to work and shape metal. There was no chance of a blacksmith's son going on the great adventure.

The morning wore on, and the blazing sun made the water sparkle like jewels and a heat haze shimmered over the surface of the waves. Daire remained on the dockside. He had found a little spot between two huge bundles of rope, where he was sheltered from the heat of the day and which was close enough to the ship so that he could watch the people coming and going.

In the early part of the afternoon, when most of the city of Murias was resting, Nuada, the King of the Tuatha De Danann, and Oghma, his brother, who had discovered the art of writing, visited the ship. They did so quietly and without fuss, but Daire, from his hiding place, could see them clearly.

Nuada, the king, was a huge man, one of the tallest men of their race. His hair was black – so black that it shone almost purple in the sunlight and he wore a simple silver band around it instead of a crown. He wore plain silver armour with a sun-wheel design on the breastplate, and there was a tall battle-axe strapped to his back.

'When do we sail?' His voice was deep and carried clearly across the waves to the young boy.

Oghma, the king's brother, shook his head. 'Soon, very soon now. Perhaps even later on today.' Oghma was smaller than his older brother, and slimmer, and his hair was already beginning to turn grey.

'Today,' Nuada said slowly. 'We must be away not later than today. We have a long journey ahead of us.' He paused and then added, 'and we haven't much time left.' He lifted his head and looked up over the town, towards the mountains.

Daire squirmed around in his hiding place and followed the direction in which the king was looking. But all he could see was the huge volcano which was called Lord Thunder.

He heard the king speak again and turned back.

'Who knows when Lord Thunder will speak again?'

His brother nodded. 'The priests and magicians say it will be soon.'

'And then?' Nuada asked.

'They say it will destroy the Isle of the Goddess,' Oghma said slowly, nervously running his fingers through his thin hair. 'They say it will bury the Four Cities beneath a covering of lava many miles deep.'

Nuada sighed. He slapped his brother on the shoulder and turned away, but his voice drifted across the waves. 'All the more reason for us to find this new land for our people.'

So, Daire thought excitedly, it was true. When the *Seeker* had discovered the new land and made it safe, then the rest of the Tuatha De Danann would join them. He looked back over his shoulder at Lord Thunder and felt his heart begin to pound. But would they be in time before the mountain spoke and threw fire and lava down onto the cities? Even as he watched a thin wisp of dark smoke drifted up from the cone into the clear blue sky.

Daire crouched back in the shadows as the king, his brother and their advisers hurried from the ship and set off in their chariots, back in the direction of the palace. Soon the ship grew quiet and the guards, now that the king had left, became more relaxed. They drifted off to one side and huddled down on the deck, out of sight, and then Daire heard the rattle of dice off the metal decks.

The young boy slipped from his hiding place and darted towards a pile of heavy wooden boxes. From there it was only a step to the water's edge. He sat down on the dockside, and hesitated for a moment, while his heart pounded painfully in his chest. This was his last chance to get aboard the *Seeker*. The idea had come to him suddenly; it was a mad, crazy, foolish idea, and he knew if he thought about it for too long he would be too frightened to act. So he didn't think. He took a deep breath and slipped down into the waves.

The water was warm and salty, and Daire's head bobbed

to the surface almost immediately. He was only a few feet away from the ship, and its huge anchor chain hung down almost by his head. But this side was closest to the guards. Daire took a deep breath and then, bending his body almost double, he dived down and under the ship.

He came up on the seaward side. He was red-faced and gasping and he clung to one of the links of the anchor chain while he caught his breath. He could see the huge sweep of the bay of Murias, with its white-washed villas and red-bricked houses lining the beaches. Higher up on the mountains that almost completely surrounded the city were the palaces of gold and silver, copper and bronze of the Lords of the Tuatha De Danann. In the early morning and late evening when the sun was low in the sky, they glowed and shimmered and the tiny diamonds set into the walls sparkled like a thousand stars. It was a very beautiful sight.

But then he swung around and looked up at the blackened sides of Lord Thunder the volcano, and he shivered to think that all this would soon be gone, buried beneath the thick lava.

Daire took a deep breath and began to climb up the huge links of the anchor chain. The chain itself was almost as thick as his own body and he found it easy to climb up along the links.

He peered over the edge of the craft. Off to the right-hand side – the starboard side, as it is called on a ship – the guards were still playing dice, and too busy to notice him. Still clinging to the edge of the deck he looked around for a hiding place.

There were a lot of large wooden boxes piled not far from him. Some were open and seemed to be packed with long bolts of cloth. Closer still there were sacks of fruit and vegetables, and beside them cases of salted meat. Daire's stomach rumbled and he realised how hungry he was. He hadn't eaten since morning.

The boy waited until the crewmen were actually rolling the dice before he heaved himself up onto the deck and rolled quickly across to the boxes and sacks. He squirmed beneath a sack of apples and wedged himself in between two boxes of fruit. The smell of the apples was almost overpowering and he took one and rubbed it on his sleeve before biting down deeply into it. It crunched so loudly that he stopped chewing in fright in case he had been heard. But then he heard the dice rattle on the deck and knew it was safe.

Daire settled back against the rough sacking to finish off his apple. No one would be looking for him, he knew. His parents, who lived outside the city, had apprenticed him to one of his father's brothers who was a magician. They thought that if he managed to learn some minor spells he would be able to help them around their small farm and forge. However, his uncle, although a very kind and cheerful man, was also very forgetful. It was one of the reasons he was not a very good magician – he kept forgetting half his spells. Daire smiled to himself, his uncle probably wouldn't even notice he was missing.

His stomach rumbled again, and he reached for another apple. . .

Daire awoke suddenly. He was cold and shivering and he felt a little sick. For a moment, he didn't know where he was, but then he suddenly remembered and realised that he must have fallen asleep.

There were people moving around him, and voices calling and talking together. Daire squeezed in tighter into his little hiding place – and then he noticed that the ship was actually moving. For a single instant he was frightened, but then he smiled widely. His great adventure was under way.

He heard footsteps approaching.

'Right then, let's start moving the fruit and vegetables.' The voice was gruff and sounded slightly breathless. 'We'll shift them down there.'

And before Daire had a chance to move, the sack of apples that he was hiding behind was pulled away and he was caught in the torchlight.

'What's this?' the gruff voice roared. 'A stowaway?'

A huge hairy hand reached in for Daire, but the young boy managed to slip from under it and dart out between the man's legs... only to run straight into another man. A hand clamped down on his shoulder holding him tight.

'What's going on here, eh?' The second voice was softer and gentler, and Daire thought it sounded familiar.

'A stowaway, sire.'

Sire, Daire thought. But only kings were called *sire*... He looked up into the face of Nuada, King of the Tuatha De Danann. 'Sire,' he whispered and attempted to bow, but the king was still holding onto his shoulder.

'Are you indeed a stowaway?' Nuada asked him gently.

Daire could only nod.

'Why?'

The boy looked up into the king's hard grey eyes. Like most of the Tuatha De Danann race, they were slightly slanted, and looked huge in his long, thin face.

'Why?' the king asked again.

Daire shrugged uncomfortably. 'I wanted to come with you,' he said. 'That's all.' He paused and then added, 'Have we come far, sire?'

'Too far to return,' the king said. 'Will your parents not be worried?'

'I am apprenticed to a magician with a very bad memory,' Daire said. 'They won't even know I've gone, and I don't think he will either.'

Nuada nodded slowly. 'Well, we're stuck with you now. But what are we to do with you?'

'I have some skill in metal-working and my father is related to Goibniu the Blacksmith...'

Nuada smiled. 'Ah. Well then, I think you shall be the Smith's apprentice.' He looked over Daire's shoulder. 'Laeg, see this lad is fed, and then bring him to the Smith.' He turned back to Daire. 'This may be a long voyage: I'm sure I shall see you again.' He nodded and turned away. The young boy and the crewman both bowed deeply.

Laeg straightened up and looked down at Daire. He saw a young boy of about ten years old, with thick black hair and sharp, bright eyes. He was wearing a none too clean tunic that was held around the middle by a broad leather belt. 'I suppose the first thing to do is to get you fed,' Laeg said kindly. He was a huge bear of a man with copper-coloured skin, a head of bright red frizzled hair and a beard to match. He was not of the De Danann people, Daire realised, but was one the Fir Dearg, the Red Men, from the forests that lay to the west of the Four Cities.

'I am a little hungry,' Daire said. 'All I've had is a few...'

'Apples,' Laeg smiled. He ran his thumb across the boy's sticky chin. 'I can see that. And when we have you fed,' he added, 'we'd better get you washed up. We can't have you meeting the famous Goibniu with a dirty face, now, can we?'

Daire nodded uncertainly. 'What's he like?' he asked, following Laeg as he made his way towards the kitchen, or the galley, as it was called on a ship.

The Red Man looked over his shoulder and smiled. 'Och, but he's a terrible man, a terrible man altogether.'

Daire met Goibniu later that evening. The Smith had been given the huge space below deck for his tools and equipment, and when Laeg led Daire down below, the young boy's first impression was of a huge cave with walls of metal. It was badly lit too, with only a few glowing bowls of light scattered here and there, sparkling off the gold walls, and sending dancing shadows across the mysterious bundles that were piled everywhere. In a far distant corner someone was whistling tunelessly and gently tapping a long bar of metal.

Laeg nodded. 'That's Goibniu. I'll leave you here – and remember, don't let him bully you.'

'I won't.'

The Red Man nodded. 'I'll wait for you above.'

Daire approached the pool of light cautiously. He was beginning to get a little frightened now – he had heard such terrible tales about the famous man who had discovered metal and how it could be heated, shaped and twisted into everything from a pot to a sword to a ship. Goibniu – what a strange name, Daire thought, even for the De Danann, but then the Smith wasn't a true De Danann. His mother was from the People of the Goddess, but his father was one of the Fir Dearg. Daire tried to walk on his toes, his footsteps sounding very loud on the metal decks.

The gentle hammering stopped.

Daire stopped also, feeling his heart beginning to pound.

'I don't want an apprentice!' The voice was rough, like two stones rubbing together, and Daire jumped with fright.

'Do you hear me? I don't want an apprentice. You'll drop things and lose things and probably burn yourself – or me, for that matter. So you can go away!'

'I won't drop things,' Daire said, angry at the man he couldn't see yet. 'My father is a smith – and a good one too, probably as good as you – and I've never dropped anything on him; nor have I ever lost anything, and I've certainly never burned anyone.'

'Yes... well.' There was a cough. 'I still don't want an apprentice.'

'Nuada said I was to be your apprentice!' Daire said, coming a few steps closer.

'Nuada knows nothing about working metal,' Goibniu snapped.

'But I do,' Daire said.

'Do you? Do you really? the Smith asked. 'Come here then.'

The boy walked into the circle of light. He gasped with surprise when he saw the Smith. Goibniu was only a little taller than himself, but he was broad, with huge bulging muscles beneath his reddish coloured skin. However, his hair was black, and his eyes were slightly slanted, and both his ears and chin came to a point. His eyes were green, and very, very bright.

The Smith pointed to the workbench before him. His thumb was almost as thick as Daire's wrist. 'Tell me what that is?' He nudged a bar of metal with his finger.

Daire picked it up and turned to the light. It was the colour of butter and was silky smooth to the touch. He ran his finger-nail along it.

'It's gold,' he said.

Goibniu said nothing, and just pointed to another piece. 'And that?'

'That's silver,' the boy said without hesitation.

'And that?' Goibniu nodded to a third piece.

Daire looked closely at it. In the reddish light from the oil lamps it was difficult to make out its true colour. 'It looks like silver,' he said at last, 'but I'm not sure.'

'You're wrong,' Goibniu said quietly, picking up the smooth bar. 'It's called white gold.'

'Oh. Does that mean you won't take me?' Daire asked.

Goibniu shrugged his huge shoulders. 'Well, you did know the other two. . .' he began.

'And my father is your cousin. . . or perhaps a second cousin,' the boy added.

'Well then, in that case you're almost a relative,' the Smith said. 'You can be my apprentice.' He smiled broadly, and Daire noticed that one of his teeth was made of gold.

'When do I start?'

'Right now,' Goibniu said. 'There's a pile of new swords over there that need polishing, and when you've finished that, you can fill up the oil lamps and check the fire.' He paused and then added, 'What's your name, boy? I don't think we were ever properly introduced.'

'My name is Daire.'

'Daire,' the Smith nodded. 'And you can call me Goibniu, or Master.'

'Yes, Master Goibniu.'

The Smith smiled hugely again. 'I think we'll get along fine,' he said.

The Seeker continued to sail south for seven days and seven nights. When the wind died down, the Lords of the Tuatha De Danann would gather and call up a magic wind, which

MONDAY
TUESDAY
WEDNESDAY
THURSDAY
FRIDAY
SATURDAY
SUNDAY

would push them on.

However, on the seventh day a storm wind began to blow. Dark, heavy clouds gathered on the horizon, and flurries of rain and sleet rattled across the metallic decks, and some of the more experienced sailors promised that the coming storm would be a terrible one.

The crew hurried about tying everything down, and Goibniu had Daire return all the loose bars of metal back to their heavy wooden boxes, and locked up all the tools so that they wouldn't be thrown about when the storm finally broke. The Smith then left the young boy while he went to a meeting with the rest of the De Danann lords.

Daire had just about finished tidying up when the Smith returned. The small man was red-faced and excited. 'We must clear a space in the centre of the floor,' he said breathlessly. 'All the Lords are going to work a piece of High Magic.'

'What's High Magic?' Daire asked.

'The oldest kind. The magic that came into this world when the world was made. It is the most powerful. Now, hurry, hurry, we must clear a space. They'll be here soon.'

'I'll get some help,' Daire said, and quickly ran up the ladder onto the deck.

'There you are! I haven't seen you for a while, young man.'

Daire recognised the gruff voice and spun around. 'Laeg!' he said with a smile.

The Red Man smiled. He nodded below decks. 'How's he treating you?'

'Oh, he's good to me.'

'You're not letting him bully you, are you?'

Daire smiled. 'I don't think he could if he tried; he's too kind-hearted. But Laeg,' he said, 'you must help me. The Lords will be gathering shortly to work some High Magic, and we need some help to clear the floor below.'

The Red Man nodded. 'I'll help you.'

Between them, they soon had the deck clear, and just as they were finishing, Goibniu returned with a tall, black-haired, sharp-faced woman. She glanced at Laeg and Daire, but ignored them.

'Who was that?' Daire whispered.

'That is Morrigan, the Warrior. You've seen her soldiers about the deck surely?'

'Their crest is a black crow on a white circle?'

Laeg nodded. 'That's them.' He nodded in the direction Morrigan and Goibniu had gone. 'Be careful of her, she's a very dangerous woman. And now, I'd better go; the rest of the Lords will soon be here.'

'Should I go?' Daire asked.

The Red Man considered. 'No. You're the Smith's apprentice. You should stay here, in case he wants you – but stay out of sight until you're called.'

'Thank you, Laeg, for all the help,' Daire said.

The Red Man smiled and nodded. He then turned and hurried up the ladder onto the deck, while Daire found himself a spot in amongst the boxes where he was safely out of the way, but close enough if his Master wanted him.

Soon, the De Danann lords began to arrive. Nuada arrived first, his silver armour shining red in the light of the many oil lamps. His brother Oghma arrived shortly afterwards, followed by old Diancecht, the famous magician and physician who had discovered the art of healing. Brigit came in with him. She too was a great healer and the finest poet in the Land of the De Danann.

Then two women moved quietly down the steps, and Morrigan moved out of the shadows to join them. The three women were very alike, as if they were sisters. There was Badb, the Lady of Battle, a tall white-haired, pale faced woman, who wore plain black armour, and beside her stood Macha, who was sometimes called the Raven, because she was so dark.

The last to arrive was Manannan. He was not truly of the De Danann people but was said to be the last of an older race, and was sometimes called the Lord of the Sea. His hair and beard had a greenish tinge and even his skin was slightly greenish. His eyes, like those of fish, never blinked. He was also able to breathe under water and was said to be able to raise up storms, and control the winds.

When everyone had arrived, they gathered in the centre of the room in a rough circle. Nuada stepped into the circle, and raised his hands for silence.

'I thank you all for coming,' he began. 'I have asked you here so that we can join together and work some of the Old High Magic. My lord Manannan tells me that the storm that is fast approaching is very powerful, and that even with our magic defences it will still damage us beyond repair.'

'What do you wish to do, brother?' Oghma asked quietly.

Nuada smiled, his eyes flashing brightly in the light of the torches. 'I wish to raise this craft above the storm!'

'Above the storm?' Goibniu rumbled. 'What do you mean?'

The king raised his arm and pointed upwards. 'We're going to fly!'

The king stepped back out of the circle, and then he joined hands with Oghma and Diancecht who stood on either side of him. They in turn joined hands with the persons standing beside them and soon all the lords of the Tuatha De Danann were joined together.

Daire, watching intently from his hiding place, saw them all bow their heads and then they began to sing in their own secret language. He saw the oil lamps begin to flicker and then dim, and soon he could barely make out their shapes in the darkness.

Suddenly the voices stopped. Daire shivered. He felt cold and the air tasted damp. He looked around, but could see nothing. But when he looked back at the circle of the De Danann, he saw that they were each outlined in a glowing circle of dull blue-green light. They began to chant again and then the light began to spin and revolve around the circle, growing brighter all the time.

And then it began to move upwards.

Daire felt the *Seeker* tremble and then it too moved – as if it had been pulled up and out of the water. Slowly, very slowly, the glowing circle of light moved up around the bodies of the lords, and as it moved higher, so too did Daire have the feeling that the ship was also moving upwards. When the blue circle of light had reached head-level it stopped and so too did the feeling of movement.

The De Danann lords stopped their singing and chanting and then, without saying a word, the circle broke up and they filed out one by one, until only Goibniu was left alone. He looks very tired and old, Daire thought as he slowly straightened up and stepped out of his hiding place.

The Smith looked up. For a moment he looked angry, but then he smiled. 'Don't let the others know that you saw what happened,' he said quietly.

'I thought you might need me,' Daire said.

Goibniu nodded. 'You can blow out the lamps,' he said. 'I'm tired now, I'm going to rest for a while. Magic is very exhausting.'

'Have we really moved upwards?' Daire asked. 'Are we really flying?'

The Smith shrugged. 'I suppose we are. We're probably flying above the storm clouds. When the storm is over then we'll go down to the sea again.'

Morning came and Daire went about his usual duties of feeding the animals and cleaning out their cages. It wasn't really his job; Laeg was supposed to do it, but the boy had offered because he loved animals. He shivered in the thick fog that covered the ship. It was cold and damp and so dense that it was difficult to see anything that was more than an arm's length away. He had attempted to look over the side to see if they were actually flying, but he could see nothing in the fog.

It stayed like that all day. And the next day and the next day and the next, and so on for over a week with no sign of a change. On the morning of the eighth day, Daire was once again looking after the animals and birds when he heard voices in the fog quite close to him. He recognised the voices as belonging to the king and his brother.

'I cannot understand it,' Nuada said, 'we should be near land, and yet we've no way of telling.'

'Can we not use some magic to help us?' Oghma asked.

'Manannan has warned me against using any sort of magic. He says the land we are nearing is inhabited by demons who are able to smell magic. We don't want to warn them.'

'Then how are we going to find the land?'

The king and his brother loomed up out of the shadows before Daire. 'I don't know,' Nuada said, and then he spotted the boy. 'Hello. I knew we would see one another again.'

Daire bowed deeply to the two De Danann lords. Nuada and Oghma bowed slightly and were about to move on when Daire looked up into their faces. 'My lords...' he said slowly, and then he stopped.

Nuada knelt down on the deck beside him. 'Yes... Daire, isn't it?'

'Yes, my lord.'

'What were you about to say?' Nuada asked.

'My lord, if we cannot find the land ourselves, why can we not let something else find it for us?' Daire said excitedly.

The king shook his head. 'I'm not sure what you mean.'

'You said that we were close to the land?'

'Very close indeed.'

'Well, my lord, there is a hive of bees here,' Daire began. He saw the king beginning to frown and hurried on. 'What if we were to let them go – and then follow them. Don't you see? – they would head straight for the nearest grass and flowers.'

Nuada looked over his shoulder at his brother. 'What do you think?'

Oghma nodded slowly. 'I think it might just work,' he said. 'Yes, I think it might just work.'

Nuada straightened up suddenly. 'We'll try it now. Gather the De Danann here. And you,' he turned to Daire, 'prepare that hive of bees.'

The lords of the Tuatha De Danann gathered quickly, and

the crew of the *Seeker* slipped away from their duties and climbed up into the slack rigging to look down on what was happening. They were all tense and curious, wondering why the king had called them together so early in the day.

Nuada raised his hands for silence. The fog gathered on his silver armour in tiny beads which shimmered and shook as he moved. 'This won't take long,' he said loudly, but the fog muffled his voice and those at the back had to strain to make out what he was saying.

'This is Daire,' he said. 'Most of you will remember he is the stowaway we found the day we set sail. He has been the Smith's apprentice since then, and Goibniu tells me he is an excellent pupil. However,' he continued, 'we think he may have discovered a quick way to bring us to our new land.' He stepped back and laid his hand on Daire's shoulder. 'Tell them what you told me,' he said softly.

'*Me!*' the boy whispered loudly.

'Yes, you,' the king smiled. 'It was your idea.' He urged Daire forward gently.

The boy bowed briefly to the De Danann lords. His great idea suddenly didn't seem so good now with all those stern faces and hard eyes staring at him, but then he caught sight of Laeg's red hair and beard at the back of the crowd. The Red Man nodded at him and then winked. Suddenly Daire felt much better.

'My idea,' he said loudly, but he coughed and had to start again. Someone in the crowd laughed. 'My idea,' he continued, 'is to release the swarm of bees we have on board with us. Their senses are much more sensitive than ours and they will be sure to head straight for the nearest grass and flowers. All we have to do is to follow them,' he finished in a rush.

There was a moment's silence and then someone in the crowd began to clap. Soon everyone, including the lords and ladies of the De Danann were clapping.

Diancecht the physician stepped forward. He looked at the boy with his sharp, piercing eyes. 'It is a brilliant idea,' he

said in his quiet way. 'Simple, but brilliant.' He looked closely at Daire. 'If you ever get tired of being the Smith's apprentice you can always become mine,' he added. The physician then looked at Nuada. 'When do we try this excellent idea?'

The king shrugged. 'How about right now?' he said.

Diancecht nodded. 'Right now it is then.'

The crewmen scurried to their places, while the De Danann lords took up their positions below deck, so that they could work their High Magic and bring the craft down. Only Morrigan the warrior-woman remained on deck beside Daire, because she had the sharpest eyesight and would be able to follow the flight of the bees.

When all was in readiness, Daire took hold of the big wicker basket and stepped forward into the prow of the *Seeker*. He could feel his heart pounding against the wood of the basket as he set it down on the golden deck. He then took a deep breath and slowly and carefully eased the top off.

For a moment nothing happened, and then a loud and angry buzzing came from inside. The buzzing grew louder until even the wood was vibrating and then, in one solid mass, like a thick cloud, the swarm of bees took off. They spun around over Daire's head for a few moments, and he didn't even breathe, nor was he stung, and then they shot out over the prow of the *Seeker* and down into the fog.

Morrigan darted forward and leaned out so far over the rail that Daire was afraid she might fall out. She called aloud in the secret language he had heard them use before, and the ship tilted downwards slightly, and increased speed. Again and again, Morrigan shouted directions, sometimes bringing the *Seeker* down, sometimes a little to the left or right as the swarm of bees changed direction.

And suddenly it was all over.

Morrigan shouted aloud in surprise as the *Seeker* broke through the clouds and they found that they were hovering just above a smooth and grassy plain. To one side the sea crashed onto a rocky beach and, on the other side, low hills rose into mountains. The land seemed green and fertile and stretched as far as the eye could see.

And the grassy plain was dotted with flowers on which the bees were feeding happily.

Nuada came up and laid his hand on Daire's shoulder. 'Well, what are you going to call this place? It was your idea after all.'

Daire looked down over the side of the *Seeker* at the huge green plain covered with flowers. 'I would like to call it the Plain of Honey,' he said softly.

Nuada nodded. 'Then that's what we'll do, but we'll use the old language of the De Danann, and call it *Mag Mell.*' He turned to the crew and the De Danann lords. 'This will be the new home for our people. Let's cheer its discoverer...'

And that is how the People of the Goddess, the magical Tuatha De Danann, came to the Land of Erin.

The Departure of The Tuatha De Danann: The Secret Places

The Tuatha De Danann ruled the land of Erin wisely and well for many, many years, and they used their great gifts for good. But in the end new invaders came from the south. These were the Milesians, and they brought with them a terrible weapon – iron.

The De Danann people were defeated at the great battle of Tailltiu, for their magic could not overcome the iron swords and spears of the newcomers.

And so the Tuatha De Danann departed from the World of Men and went to their Secret Places. . .

'We are now the last of our race in this land,' the old man said slowly, looking around him at the deserted village. In the grey light of the dawn, with the morning mist still clinging to the stones, the round houses looked very lonely.

'But we're not really leaving,' his son said quickly.

Faolan, the old man, shook his head sadly. 'We were once kings in this land – and now we are nothing.' He picked up his long staff and stepped out into the deserted street. Donn, his son, took one last look back at his home, and then followed him.

They moved slowly and sadly down the street to the stream where the rest of the village had gathered with their goods and belongings. There were only a few people there, not more than twenty. Many had gone to fight in the war with the Milesians, but only a few had returned.

Faolan, the village elder, raised his hand for silence. He was an old, old man now, his hair and beard snow-white and his face creased with lines. He had come to Erin on the *Seeker,* the ship which had carried the first of the People of the Goddess to this place.

'You all know why we are here,' he said very softly, although, in the quiet of the morning, his voice carried clearly. 'The armies of our people have been defeated, and many of our leaders are dead. As you know, we must leave this world.'

'But our homeland is destroyed,' one of the villagers said. 'The Four Cities are now lost beneath the waves.'

Faolan nodded. 'We are leaving this world – but we are not leaving Erin,' he said quietly.

'I don't understand,' the same villager said.

Donn stepped forward. 'What my father means,' he said quickly, 'is that the Lords of the De Danann have prepared new homelands for us – "Secret Places" they are called. They have created huge caves under the ground for us to live in. These will be called forts and they are magical; they have their own light and heat and we will be able to grow whatever we will need.'

'Also,' his father added, 'we will never grow old there. We will be immortal.'

'So you see,' Donn said, 'although we are leaving this world, we are not truly leaving Erin. We will continue to live beneath the ground in our forts.'

'But will we be able to return to this world?' someone asked.

Faolan nodded. 'These forts will look like rounded hills from above, but there will be a door in these hills, and, on certain evenings, we will be able to ride out into the World of Men again.'

The villagers murmured amongst themselves for a while and then one stepped out of the crowd. He was a small, dark-skinned man, looking more like one of the Fir Dearg than one of the De Danann.

'And what happens if someone doesn't want to go into this fort?' he asked.

'No one is forcing you, Lugh,' Faolan said. 'If you go there and find you do not like it, you will be free to leave.'

'I don't think I want to go and live underground,' Lugh said, almost to himself. He shifted his hammer on his shoulder, and rubbed his other hand on his thick blacksmith's apron.

'But you'll have to go into hiding then,' Donn said. 'You cannot allow yourself to be caught by any man.'

'I won't be caught,' Lugh said confidently, 'and sure, even if I am, I can always escape.'

Faolan shook he is head sadly. 'I'm sorry you're not coming with us, Lugh. We'll all miss you. However,' he added, 'you won't be alone, because there are people in some of the other

villages like you who do not wish to live underground. Surprisingly, a lot of them – like you – are either blacksmiths or have some Fir Dearg blood in them. Perhaps you could all join together.'

Lugh nodded. 'Aye, perhaps we could.'

'But a word of warning,' Faolan said. 'Be careful not to hide all your wealth in one place in case you are caught. Spread it around in a dozen different places. Try and travel only at night, and wear clothes that will blend in with the trees and grass or the flowers if it is summer.'

The small man nodded. 'Thank you for your advice. I will remember it.'

Faolan smiled. 'And we will remember you when we need something mended.' The old man then turned back to the rest of the villagers. 'We must go now.' He raised his arm and pointed into the sky towards the east, 'Look, the sun is rising. Take a good look at it – it is the last sunrise you will ever see.'

The Tuatha De Danann then mounted their tall, thin, horses, with the children on smaller ponies and, with Donn in the lead, they set off at a gallop into the west. Faolan was the last to leave. He sat on his horse and looked around and there were tears in his eyes. Then he nodded to Lugh and turned his horse into the west.

The small dark man watched the Tuatha De Danann ride from this world. Soon they would become a myth, he knew. What he didn't know was that soon he, and the others like him who had not gone with the De Danann, would also become a legend. For they would later be called Leprechauns.

The Fairy Horses

When the Sidhe left this world and retreated to their secret places, they sometimes allowed their horses and cows to roam free to graze in the fields of men. Now the horses were the finest in the world, fine-boned, fast as the wind and very intelligent. Usually humans only saw them from a distance, or at dead of night, their coats shining silver in the moonlight. People often tried to catch them, but very few succeeded – and those who did manage to capture one of the fairy horses usually found that they brought nothing but bad luck.

This is a story about a young prince of Erin long ago who managed to catch one of those horses. . .

Fintan led his mother down the stone steps of the palace and out beyond the high walls into the fields. The prince stopped and pointed down towards the lake that bordered the fields. 'Look,' he said.

Queen Scota shaded her eyes with her hand. She was a tall, thin woman with long flowing hair that had once been gold but which was now streaked with silver. As Fintan watched, he saw his mother's face change expression and harden, and her blue eyes grew cold and angry.

'Who has done this?' she demanded.

Fintan looked down over the fields again and shook his head. From where he was standing he could see that the field that bordered the lake, which should have been a mass of waving golden corn was muddy and trampled, the corn crushed and scattered. He shook his head. 'I don't know,' he said at last. Although he was only twelve, he was almost as tall as his mother and he had her golden hair and sharp blue eyes.

'Who first discovered that the field had been destroyed?' the queen demanded.

'I did,' Fintan said, 'when I was going down to swim in the lake earlier this morning.'

The queen turned on her heel and stalked back towards the palace gate, her long green gown billowing out behind her. 'Fetch me the Captain of the Guard,' she called back to Fintan.

The young boy nodded. He stood for a few moments looking at the field of destroyed corn and then he hurried off to the barracks to find Colman, the Captain of the Palace Guard.

The long high throne room was dark and the only light came from a roaring log and turf fire and a few scattered torches set into the wall. Queen Scota was standing in front of the fire, her head bowed and with her hands clasped in front of her, her foot tapping impatiently. She looked up when she heard the footsteps approaching.

'Well?' she demanded as her son and the Captain of the Guard hurried into the smoky room.

Colman MacGregan stopped and bowed. He was a tall warrior from Erin's wild western shores, and he had the black hair and hard black eyes of his people. 'Your majesty wished to see me?' he said in his soft, almost musical accent.

'Have you seen the field?' Queen Scota snapped.

'I have,' Colman said quietly.

'That is part of next year's harvest – and it has been ruined. I want to know what happened; I want to know who did it. I also want to know what you are going to do about it?'

Colman straightened the heavy woollen cloak on his shoulders, and then rested his left hand on the bronze knife in his belt. 'I have looked at the damage with Prince Fintan,' he said, 'and we have found the imprints of horses' hooves in the soft earth by the water's edge.'

Queen Scota rested both hands on her hips and asked in astonishment, 'And how did riders get this close to the palace? Where were the guards?' she suddenly shouted.

The Captain of the Guard smiled. 'I said horses, your majesty, I did not say that there had been riders.'

The queen took a step closer, her eyes flashing angrily. 'Just what do you mean?' she demanded.

'There is no way any riders could have approached so close to the palace without the guards first seeing them. Therefore,' he concluded, 'the horses must have either come from the palace – or from the lake!'

'From the lake!' the queen gasped, a cold shiver running up her spine.

Fintan nodded. 'I have looked at the prints on the ground, mother,' he said, 'the hoof-marks are thinner and finer than our own horses.'

The queen shook her head doubtfully, but then Fintan took a gleaming half-circle from his tunic. He held it up and the light from the fire turned it red-gold. 'What is it?' she asked.

'It's a horse-shoe,' Fintan said softly, turning the piece of metal around in his hands, 'And it's made of solid silver!'

The queen held out her hand and took the piece of metal from Fintan. She stepped back to the fire and examined it more closely. It was indeed a horse-shoe, but the workmanship was far finer than any her own blacksmiths were able to make, and the hoof it was made for was far smaller and neater than a normal horse. She handed the shoe back to her son and then looked at Colman. 'Well, what do you think happened?'

'I think we're dealing with Aug... Augh.' He turned to Fintan. 'What are they called?' he asked.

'Aughisky,' the prince said, 'water-horses.'

Colman nodded. 'Aye, water-horses. There must be a Sidhe palace beneath the waters of the lake,' he said. 'If they are short of fodder in the Otherworld, they will allow their creatures to roam free to find their own food. Naturally they would have headed straight for our fields.'

'Are you sure?' Queen Scota asked.

'It has happened in other parts of the country.'

'Well, it's not going to happen here. I want them stopped,'

the queen snapped.

Colman shook his head. 'That might not be so easy.'

'I want them stopped,' the queen repeated.

The Captain of the Guard looked at Fintan and then back to the queen. 'We really need the help of the druids in this,' he said, 'but unfortunately most of them are on the Isle of Mona for some secret ceremony, and we'll have to wait a few days.'

'I want them stopped – tonight!' Queen Scota said. 'If any more fields are destroyed, my people will go hungry next winter... and I will not allow that. Stop those animals!' She turned on her heel and swept from the room.

Colman shook his head and looked at the prince. 'It's very easy for her to say she wants them stopped tonight – but she doesn't tell us how we are going to stop them, does she?'

Fintan looked at the silver horse-shoe in his hand. 'We'll find a way,' he said confidently.

That night the moon shone from a cloudless sky, and turned the black waters of the lake into a silver sheet. There was a gentle breeze and the heads of corn whispered and rustled together. The dozen men hidden amongst the stalks tried to stay as quiet as possible, but the corn cut and poked and prodded and almost drove them mad. Every time they moved the corn stalks would find another place to pinch.

Prince Fintan and Colman were hidden in a thick clump of bushes off to one side of the field, close to the water's edge. Like the rest of the men, they were holding lengths of rope – they were going to try and capture some of the horses.

'Will they come tonight?' the prince asked the Captain of the Guard.

Colman shrugged. 'I don't know, but I hope so.'

'Do you think we will be able to catch one?'

The older man shrugged again. 'I don't know – and I'm not sure I want to capture one. We should have waited until the druids returned and got some advice from them.'

Fintan nodded. He too would have liked to have waited

until the wise men had returned from their secret island. They might have been able to cast some spell that would have kept the horses from their fields, but his mother was very impatient.

'Also,' Colman added, 'what do we do if we do manage to capture one of the creatures?'

Fintan shook his head. He wasn't sure.

The night wore on and the moon rose higher in the sky, and soon the watchers began to nod off. Around about midnight, the flat, silver surface of the lake was disturbed by a ripple. It spread out in a growing black circle, and then it was joined by another and then another, and then a silver horse's head rose from the lake in a splash of water. Flat mirror-like eyes stared across the lake towards the darkened fields and long thin ears topped with wiry strands of hair twitched.

And slowly, slowly, the fairy-horse rose from the lake. It was tall and thin, its coat gleaming silver in the moonlight and its mane and tail were like silver-threads. Its feet were tiny, impossibly small to carry the weight of the creature. It stood on the surface of the water and waited.

Another horse rose up like some huge bubble, and then it was joined by another and then another of the creatures, and then, in an enormous ripple, a dozen horses rose together. They were almost identical, except that the first horse seemed to be somehow nobler than all the rest.

The fairy steeds stood on the water for a few moments while the ripples died on the lake. When the water was still again, they moved forward, trotting nimbly and daintily, their feet barely breaking the surface, the water splashing silver and black in the moonlight. They came out of the lake and climbed up the little bank and into the field of corn where they began to graze.

They passed within a few inches of Colman and Fintan, but the man and boy waited until the creatures had moved out into the field and had begun to feed and then, slowly and carefully, they crept from their hiding place.

Colman moved as close to one of the horses as possible and began to slowly swing the rope he held around his head. It made a gentle shussing sound as it spun and immediately all the fairy horses stopped feeding and their heads came up with their long ears twitching. One spotted the captain and neighed a warning. All heads turned in his direction and then suddenly the fairy-mounts scattered.

The men rushed from their hiding places and attempted to catch them. But the horses were too fast and too cunning. They dodged, twisted and turned. Once or twice they darted straight towards the men, only turning aside at the last moment when the men had leaped for cover.

One by one, they splashed into the water and disappeared beneath the dark waves.

Soon, only one horse remained, and he was the creature that had appeared first. He had dashed about the field, charging towards the men, rearing up on his hind legs, protecting the other horses and allowing them to make their escape. But when they had all vanished into the lake, he neighed triumphantly and then dashed towards the water himself.

The guards ran at him and flung their ropes, but most fell

short or just slid off his polished back. And then Prince Fintan rose up out of the tall rushes that grew by the waters edge directly in front of him. The rope in his hand was spinning around his head so fast that it was almost invisible. The fairy horse didn't see him until it was too late. It attempted to change direction, but the ground beneath its feet was soft and it slipped – and while it was attempting to find its balance, Fintan managed to drop the rope around its head.

The fairy horse froze in astonishment and then it lifted its head and neighed – but not like any normal horse. This was an almost human-like cry, and it echoed and re-echoed across the flat waters of the lake. It reared up on its hind legs and the prince, who was still holding tightly onto the rope, was dragged up off his feet. The horse shook its head and Fintan was tossed to and fro and was nearly thrown off. But then Colman and the rest of the guards raced up and, while the captain grabbed the prince's rope and helped pull the horse's head down, the guards flung their ropes around the creature's neck and body. The horse struggled for a few moments, but then it gave an almost human sigh and stood still. It turned its huge, cat-like eyes on Fintan and stared hard at him. The prince shivered suddenly.

'It looks like it's trying to say something to me,' he said to Colman.

'Aye,' the captain nodded, 'it does. I think your mother should let this creature go before it brings bad luck to us all.'

'But she won't do that,' the prince said.

Colman nodded again. 'I know.' He then turned from the horse and looked at Fintan. 'But a word of warning, prince. Stay away from this creature – and never, never ride it.'

The prince looked from the Captain of the Guard and then back to the fairy horse, and he shivered again. 'I won't,' he promised.

As expected, Queen Scota would not allow the horse to be set free – even when the druids returned and insisted that she should. They promised that if the horse was not allowed to go free, then the fairy folk would come and take it. . . and they would be sure to make the queen and her court pay for capturing one of their prize animals. But the queen insisted that the horse stay – while she had it, their fields were safe.

A year passed.

The horse grew, both in size and beauty. It was a lovely creature, tall, fine-boned, with a coat that looked like it was made of silver silk and a mane and tail that were as fine as silver wire. However, the horse had a vicious temper and would snap its great slab-like teeth at anyone who came too close – except for Fintan. With the prince, the horse was as gentle as a foal.

Soon the prince grew very fond of the beautiful creature, and came every day to groom and talk to it. But his mother, remembering the warning that both the druids and Colman had given her, would not allow the boy to ride the horse.

Every year, a huge fair would be held in Erin, when the merchants, artists and farmers from all parts of the country would bring their wares to be sold. The highlight of the fair was three days of games and sports. Champions would come from all parts of the country and try to win the prizes that were given for spear throwing, chariot racing, and weight lifting. But the most important event was the great horse race between the royal families of Erin. At that time there was more than one king and queen in Erin, although all the minor kings were in turn ruled by the Ard Rí, the High King.

And Fintan wanted to ride the fairy horse in the race.

'No,' the queen said, 'I cannot allow it.'

'But Capall is safe with me,' Fintan insisted. He had named the creature 'Capall,' which in the Irish language simply meant 'horse'.

'That is a fairy-horse,' his mother said, 'and no fairy horse is ever safe.' She shook her head firmly, 'No, I will not allow you to ride it.'

'But we could win!'

Queen Scota nodded. 'Yes, perhaps your horse would come in first; but I doubt if the other judges would allow you to win. They would probably say that we had cheated by using one of the fairy steeds. No,' she said again, 'Colman will ride on his own horse, Bán.'

The prince had opened his mouth to argue, but seeing the look in his mother's eyes, had closed it again without saying a word.

The day of the horse race was warm and dry and with just a slight breeze blowing in from the east, carrying on it the very, very faint smell of the sea. The fields beyond Tara were bright with tents and gently fluttering flags. Thousands of people milled about, all in their best clothes, stopping at the stalls, tasting the fruit or freshly cooked meat, or drinking the mead. There were leather workers, who would mend your belt or sandles, or make you a scabbard for your knife. There were blacksmiths who would make you a knife, or put a new shoe on your horse, or mend the wheel of your chariot. There were soothsayers who would tell your fortune. There were jugglers, dancers, bards and harpers. There were people selling and shouting, buying and laughing. All Erin was there.

The race course had been laid out and marked with red flags. It led from the field of tents, around the palace on the Hill of Tara, along the banks of the river Boyne and then back into the village of tents. The first horse to finish the long course would be the winner.

Ten horses were entered for the race and they and their riders waited nervously as the shadows crept along the ground, growing shorter as it neared midday. The race would begin at noon.

Prince Fintan crept out from behind one of the tents and then stopped. He looked around carefully, half-expecting to see his mother or one of the guards come running after him. He knew that they would soon find out that someone had taken the fairy horse from the stables – and he was the only person who could handle the animal.

But Prince Fintan was going to race the fairy horse in the race, and he was hoping that with all the fuss and excitement, no one would notice that the horse was missing until it was too late.

When it was very close to noon, the ten riders and their horses trotted up to the starting point. Fintan only knew two of them by name: Colman and a man called Ligan, who was from the north. Fintan had hidden inside one of the smaller tents, close to the starting point. The people who owned it usually left early in the morning and didn't return until sunset and he knew he would be safe there. He had smuggled Capall in just after they had left for the fair that morning.

When Fintan saw that the shadows had almost vanished, he threw a blanket over the fairy horse's back and pulled himself up onto it. The creature whickered a little, but then was quiet. Fintan urged the horse close to the tent's opening with his knees.

At exactly noon, when the sun was directly overhead and the shadows had disappeared, the starter brought his arm up – and dropped it. The race was off!

The horses set off at a steady gallop, running strongly down the long stretch that led towards the banks of the river. At the same time, Fintan dug his heels in and the fairy horse took off with a sudden lunge that sent him shooting through the tent's opening and out into the crowded field. People threw themselves to one side as the prince urged the horse forward. Some shouted and screamed as they went tumbling backwards into yet more people; stalls with fruit and vegetables went crashing to the ground, and some of the animals, the sheep, goats and pigs, stampeded causing even more chaos.

But all this was happening behind Fintan. In a few long strides the fairy horse had reached the proper race course and had set off after the other riders.

Queen Scota, who had been watching everything from a small platform, suddenly stood up. Her left arm shot out and she shouted, 'Stop him! That's the prince! Don't let him ride!'

A guardsman stepped into Fintan's path and raised his hand, but the fairy horse just kept going and the man threw himself to one side only at the very last moment.

Soon, Fintan and his fairy horse passed some of the other riders. They looked around in astonishment to see a young boy suddenly appear from behind them riding a fairy horse – and while they were doing that he passed them by! Soon, only Colman and Ligan were ahead of him, and they were racing neck and neck as they approached the river.

'Come on,' Fintan panted, 'come on, boy.' He knew if he could manage to cross the river before the other two, he would have a clear run around the Hill of Tara and back to the finishing post. 'Come on.'

Colman and Ligan pushed their horses on as they saw the sparkling blue waters of the river Boyne approach. Like the prince, they knew that the first man across the river would more than likely be the first man home. Ligan glanced over his shoulder, just to see how far behind the rest of the riders were – and almost fell off his horse with shock. Just behind him, on the most frightening horse he had ever seen, was a boy. Colman saw his startled expression and he too turned around...

'Fintan!' he gasped.

The prince waved at the Captain of the Guard with one hand. 'I'm going to win,' he called.

'No!' Colman shouted.

'I am. I am,' Fintan laughed and, with a sudden burst of speed, the fairy horse dashed between the other two horses and began to move away in the lead.

'Stop!' Colman called, but Fintan either didn't hear him, or just didn't listen. The captain turned to Ligan. 'We must stop him. That's a fairy-horse he's riding – he doesn't know what's going to happen...'

Ligan nodded. 'I'll try and cut him off,' he shouted, turning his horse to the right and heading for a narrow spot in the river where he might be able to cross and rejoin the race-course ahead of Fintan. Colman meanwhile, raced after the prince, but the magical fairy horse was faster, much faster than any mortal beast, and this was the first time in over a year since it had been allowed out for a run.

Fintan laughed aloud as he raced past Colman and Ligan. He was going to win this race! There was only the river to cross now...

The fairy horse splashed into the shallows – and stopped! Fintan was nearly thrown over its head with the shock, but just about managed to cling on by holding tightly to its mane. 'Come on, come on,' he shouted, digging his heels in and attempting to make the creature move. But the only thing that moved were the horses ears, as if it were listening to something.

'They're going to catch up,' Fintan cried and looked around, but he could only see Colman behind him, riding flat out, his arms waving. He was shouting, but the prince couldn't make out what he was saying, only the word 'water'.

Suddenly, the fairy horse moved – but not across the river and up onto the bank as he should have. Instead it began to move down river – walking on the surface of the water. Fintan shivered. This was magic and he was frightened now. He

decided he would jump into the river and swim for the banks, where he could now see Colman on one side and Ligan on the other.

But when the prince attempted to let go of the horse's silver mane, he found that his hands were stuck fast. He tried to lift his legs, but they wouldn't move.

He couldn't let go!

And when the fairy horse reached the centre of the wide river, it began to sink, slowly, slowly, slowly beneath the waves, carrying the young prince with it...

Prince Fintan was never seen again in this world. However, on dark winter nights when the moon is full, the fairy horses will sometimes come up from the quiet lakes and old rivers and feed in the fields of men. And people who have seen them say that they are led by a young boy who rides the noblest of the animals and who wears the clothes of another age.

The King's Secret

This is a strange tale which has two different endings. It is about a famous king of Ireland who was called Labhra Loingse. He had once been known as Labhra the Dumb King, because he swallowed a fieldmouse in his beer one day and was struck dumb. However, some time later he was struck a terrible blow on the back during a fight, and he coughed up the mouse – which was still alive – and he found he could talk again.

However, Labhra Loingse was unusual in another way; he had a very strange secret. . .

The king sat under the shade of an old oak tree and dangled his feet in the water. It was a very warm day and he was hot, sticky and tired. He had stripped off most of his heavy armour, wrapped it up in a bundle in his cloak and tied it to the saddle of his horse, and now he only wore a light shirt and breeches – and his heavy horned helmet.

Even on the hottest day, Labhra Loingse never removed his helmet. No one knew why, and if anyone every did find out, the king had them killed. For he had a dark and terrible secret: he had the tall, hairy ears of a horse. An old fairy woman had cursed him with them one day when he was still a young man because she had found him beating his poor horse who couldn't run any faster. She had suddenly appeared in front of him, standing beside a stone, and his horse had reared up in fright, throwing him backwards, leaving him shaken and dazed on the ground. He had looked up to find the small, grey-haired, grey-eyed, grey-clad woman staring down at him.

'You are a cruel man, Labhra Loingse,' she had said coldly.

'But it's only a horse,' Labhra had protested.

'Only a horse? Only a horse?' The old woman had smiled then, and her smile was hard and bitter. 'I do not have much power left, but I do have enough magic left to do this!' She closed her left hand into a fist and then pointed the first and little fingers at him. The king felt his head tingle and buzz and then his ears began to burn. He clapped his hands to his head – but instead of covering his own small, rounded ears, he felt the tall, thin shapes of a horse's ears. And when he looked up, the old fairy woman had gone.

The king visited many of the magicians and doctors in the land, but no one could remove the spell. They said that it was fairy magic – the oldest and most powerful magic in the world. Now this was a long time ago when both men and women wore their hair long, and Labhra Loingse allowed his to grow until it covered his horse's ears. And he always wore a horned helmet with two holes cut on the inside of the helmet, so that the tips of his ears could stick up inside the horns.

However, twice a year the king would have his hair cut, because if it grew too long people would begin to wonder what he was hiding. The barber always came from one of the furthest parts of Erin, and when he had cut the king's hair – and seen his ears – the king would have him killed before he could tell anyone his secret.

One Midsummer's Eve, the king sent his guards across his kingdom to find a barber to cut his hair. Of course, by this time there were very few barbers left in Erin and the few that remained went into hiding about this time of year in case they should be chosen to cut the king's hair. And so, the only barber they could find was a young man who worked in a tiny village in the south-west corner of Erin.

Now this young man was the only son of a widow and when the king's soldiers took him away, she travelled to Tara, where Labhra had his court, and she begged the king to spare the life of her son.

The king didn't want to, but at last he agreed, only on

condition however that the young man would keep a secret for the rest of his life. The woman swore that her son would never betray the king's confidence. The young man – whose name was Marcan – was then brought in and, when everyone had left the room, the king took off his helmet and ordered the barber to cut his hair.

Marcan had only made a few cuts when the tops of the ears appeared. He stopped cutting and carefully parted the hair, revealing the king's ears.

Labhra swivelled around in his chair and stared up at the barber. 'So now you know my secret – and you should die because you know it. But your mother has been here and she has made me swear not to kill you because you are her only son and all she has left in the world.' The king paused and then continued. 'She also said that you would keep a secret, and so I will not kill you – on the condition that you swear an oath here and now never to tell anyone what you have seen this day. Well?'

'I swear it,' Marcan said quickly. 'I will tell no living man.'

The king nodded. 'Good. Now, you may continue cutting my hair – and I will appoint you the royal barber. Twice a year you will come to the palace and cut my hair – but remember your promise...'

'I will never forget,' Marcan swore.

Because Marcan had not been killed by the king and because he had been appointed the Royal Barber, most people assumed it was because he was the best in the land, and he soon became a wealthy man and had to move to Tara where he would cut the hair of all the lords and ladies of the court.

Of course, people would often ask him why the king wore

that strange horned helmet or why he had always killed the barbers before him, but Marcan would shake his head and say he didn't know. But people didn't believe him and kept pestering him for the answer.

Soon Marcan became very depressed. He felt that if he didn't tell the secret to someone he would burst. So he went to one of the holy men of the time, a druid, and he asked him for advice. The druid asked him to repeat the oath he had sworn to the king, and Marcan said, 'I swore I would tell no living man.'

The druid then threw back his head and laughed. 'Why then, all you have to do is to go out and tell your secret to the first thing you meet, be it bird or beast, bush or tree. Your problems will then be solved.'

Marcan thanked the druid and hurried out beyond Tara's walls and stopped at the first tree he came to. He stopped and looked around and after making sure no one was near he leaned close to the bark of the tree and whispered softly, 'Labhra Loingse has horse's ears; Labhra Loingse has horse's ears.' And now, having told something his secret, Marcan went home happy and relieved and the secret never again troubled him.

However, some months later, some woodmen came along and cut down that tree and they sent it off to one of the greatest craftsmen in Erin at that time and he, in turn, made it into a harp for Craftne the Harper.

There was to be a great feast in Tara that night, and Craftne had composed a new song in celebration of the king. The great hall was silent as the harper approached. He was a small, richly dressed, fussy man and he carried his harp in a specially made leather bag slung over his shoulder.

Craftne bowed to the king and then to the assembled lords and ladies. He sat down on a low three-legged stool and slowly removed the cover from his harp. It was a beautiful instrument, tall and slim, and with tiny precious stones set into the richly polished wood. Craftne ran his long fingers down the golden strings and a delicate shivery sound drifted out over the hall. He touched the strings again and then swept his hand from one end of it to the other. The sounds it made should have been lovely – but instead, in a high-pitched squeaky voice, it shouted, *'Labhra Loingse has horse's ears. . . Labhra Loingse has horse's ears. . . Labhra Loingse has horse's ears. . .'*

Craftne dropped the harp in fright and it shattered into pieces. The king stood up so suddenly that his horned helmet fell off and, because he had just had his hair cut, his ears were exposed for all to see. The king made a grab for his helmet, but he slipped on the steps to his throne and fell to the ground and broke his neck. The strange thing was that when he died his ears turned back to normal, so everyone knew that he had been cursed by the fairies for some evil deed.

There is another ending to this tale. When Marcan whispered his secret to the tree, he was overheard by two magpies who were perched on the branches above his head. When he had gone, they flew off in two different directions and there they met two more magpies.

'Labhra Loingse has horse's ears,' they said, and then the four magpies flew off north, south, west and east, and soon they met two magpies each.

'Labhra Loingse has horse's ears,' they said, and then they all flew off in different directions. By morning all the birds of the air knew the king's secret.

Labhra Loingse woke early the following morning. He got out of bed and went to the window to watch the sun rise over his kingdom. A magpie came and perched on the window-sill and looked at the king with its hard bright eyes.

'Labhra Loingse has horse's ears,' the bird said, and the king was so shocked, both at hearing the bird speak and because it knew his secret, that he died of fright on the spot.

The Crow Goddess

*When St Patrick brought the Christian faith to Erin, the old
Celtic gods disappeared, and men soon forgot about them.
But the old gods did not die – because they are immortal and
cannot die. They are still around, and sometimes they re-
appear...*

The sudden shower of rain sent Dermot running down the
hill towards the cave for shelter. He should have brought his
heavy oilskin with him. His grandfather, who always knew
what weather was coming, had warned him that it would rain
before evening, but Dermot, standing by the door of his
house, had just laughed and run out into the sunshine.

As usual his grandfather had been right. Shortly after midday, when he had been sitting down to his lunch of bread
and milk, he had seen the first of the grey clouds appear on
top of the mountains. But it didn't start to rain until it was
almost time to head for home. The sky suddenly darkened
– and then it poured down.

Dermot dashed into the cave just as the first heavy drops
of water spattered onto the ground outside. He was a short,
stout boy, ten years old, with a wide smiling face and hair
that was always falling into his eyes. He sat with his chin
resting on his knees and watched the rain churn the earth
outside the cave into mud. Further on down the hill, he saw
the sheep moving into the shelter of stones and behind some
of the small, stunted bushes. The boy sighed: it looked like
the rain would come down for a while. Well, he would sit it
out for an hour or so, but if it showed no sign of easing up
he would have to make a run for home.

But the rain, instead of lessening, became even heavier. It

drummed off the ground and stones, and the wind, which had also grown stronger, now and then sent flurries of icy rain into the cave mouth. Very shortly, a gale was blowing, and now leaves, twigs, pieces of branches and even small stones were being tossed past the cave mouth by the wind.

Dermot shivered. It had grown cold, and he was only wearing short trousers and a light woollen jumper. He couldn't leave now – he would be soaked in seconds and would probably catch a terrible cold. He kept moving further back into the cave, but now he had his back against the cold stone wall, and he couldn't go any further. However, he knew that if he didn't appear at home for supper then his father or older brother would be sure to come looking for him.

There was a sudden gust of wind which whipped dust and dirt into the cave and then something small and black was thrown into one corner. For a moment Dermot thought it was just a leaf but then he saw that it was moving feebly. He crept closer to have a look. It was a bird; a small, bedraggled crow.

Dermot took the bird in the palm of his hand. It couldn't have been more than a few days old. It was soaking wet and some of its feathers were ruffled and some were missing. It must have been caught in the open by the storm and tossed on the wind. He turned it over carefully in his hand, checking for any cuts or signs of broken bones. Luckily, there didn't seem to be any blood and he was able to stretch its wings and rub its thin legs without any difficulty.

'What are we going to do with you then?' he asked softly, rubbing his fingers down its back. The crow's hard black eyes watched him carefully, and its beak slowly opened and closed.

'I'm not going to hurt you,' he said. He crept back to the rear of the cave and huddled in close to the wall. In the distance thunder rumbled and the dark sky was brightened almost immediately by distant lightning.

The bird seemed to shiver in his hand and Dermot suddenly realised how cold it was. He turned up the end of his

jumper and carefully wrapped the small bird in it, and then held it close to his chest.

Thunder and lightning boomed and flashed again, closer this time, and he felt the bird's tiny body twitch with fright. 'Sssh, sssh now,' he said. It was only a very young bird, and it occurred to him that it might never have heard thunder before.

As the late afternoon wore on into evening and the storm showed no sign of lessening, Dermot began to get very worried. What was going to happen if the storm continued on into the night? His father or brother would not be able to go out and look for him – and even if they could, they might walk right outside the cave and he wouldn't even see them. Besides, he didn't think the bird would last through the night without some food and heat.

He began to cry, very, very softly to himself.

He might have fallen asleep – he wasn't sure. He did remember resting his head on his knees and closing his eyes, and at that time it had been dusty grey outside. When he raised his head from his knees it was totally black.

And then he blinked and blinked again, for he suddenly realised that he could see – even though it was night outside! The light was very dim, and was slightly greenish, but he could clearly make out the walls of the cave, and the little lichens and rock plants that clung to the stone, and he could even see his own grubby knees. The bird! He reached for the tiny crow – but it had gone.

'Do not worry yourself, the winged-one is safe!'

The voice came out of nowhere and seemed to echo inside his head. It sounded like that of a woman. 'Do not be frightened, human, I will not harm you.'

Dermot looked around, but he could see no one.

'Who... who are you?' he whispered, his voice sounding strained and cracked. 'Where are you?'

The air in front of the cave mouth seemed to shimmer, as if he were looking at it through a heat-haze, and then he found he could make out the shape of a woman. The image was blurry and indistinct. He bit his lip and said nothing.

'I am Morrigan,' the image said, and it suddenly hardened, and he found he was facing a tall, thin-faced woman wearing ancient-looking black leather armour and holding a tall battle-axe.

Dermot squeezed his eyes shut, thinking the image would go away when he opened them again, but when he did she was still there. He looked closely at her thin face, high cheek-bones and slanting eyes, and he thought he could make out pointed ears beneath her thick black hair, and then he recognised her as one of the *Sidhe*, the fairy folk.

'What. . . what do you want?' he managed to whisper.

The terrifying woman smiled, and her dark eyes lit up as if from within. 'I have come to help you,' she said.

'To help me?'

Morrigan nodded. 'I am – I was – the Goddess of War and Battles when the Tuatha De Danann ruled this land. But when the Sons of Mil came, we knew that our time was done and we left this world. And then the faith of the Christians was brought to this island by the small Roman, Patrick, and people no longer worshipped the old gods and we faded away. But we live still,' she added suddenly. 'I had another name,' Morrigan continued. She held out her hand and in it the small black crow nestled comfortably, looking plump and healthy. 'I was called the Crow Goddess.'

Dermot blinked. He had heard his grandfather tell some of the ancient legends about the terrible Crow Goddess. He felt his throat tighten. 'You said you wanted to help me. . .'

Morrigan nodded. 'You helped one of my creatures, so too will I help you. Close your eyes,' she commanded.

Dermot squeezed his eyes shut. There was a rushing sound, like wind, and then he suddenly felt warmer and he realised that the sound had changed. When he opened his eyes he found he was in the barn behind his own house. . .

Dermot's family did not want to believe him when he told them about the Crow Goddess. But there was no other way that he could have been suddenly transported from the cold cave nearly five miles away to his own home except by magic, now was there?

The Fairies' Revenge

The fairy folk are strange people. They can be nice and kind one day, and then mean and spiteful the next. If you are good to them, they will give you anything you desire, and yet, if you anger one of them, they can make things miserable for you. But if you do happen to know one of the Sidhe, *you must remember never to tell a lie about them.*

Red Rory – or Rory Dearg as he was called because of his bright red hair – knew some of the sea-fairies. He was always good and kind to them and in return they helped him in many ways. But when he told a lie about them, they were very angry. . .

One evening in late September Rory Dearg and a few of his friends were sitting on the long pebbled beach tossing stones into the foaming waves. They were talking about the fairy folk, the *Sidhe.*

'They live in those caves over there,' Rory said, pointing out across the sea towards a small rocky island. Rory was a short, stout man, with a head of bright red hair and bushy eyebrows.

'How do you know?' Thomas, one of his neighbours, asked.

'Because I'm very friendly with the fairy folk,' Rory said proudly. He took a deep breath and smiled broadly. 'They often come over here and visit their relations that live in the fairy mounds.'

'And how do they get over here?' another neighbour asked.

Rory stood up and pointed down into the sea. 'There's a secret path, made of white sand and coral that runs along the sea bed from the island to the mainland,' he said.

'How do you know?' the neighbour asked.

Rory smiled again, his broad face breaking up into hundreds of tiny wrinkles. 'Because I've walked along that road with them.'

'You! What would the *Sidhe* folk want you for?'

'Why, to help carry their sacks of gold and silver across to their relations. They make it on the island, but because it's so heavy, they usually ask me to carry it for them.'

'And do they pay you?' Thomas asked.

'Of course they do,' Rory said.

'Well, let's see some fairy gold or silver then,' Thomas said.

Rory Dearg smiled secretively, 'Oh, it's neither gold nor silver that they pay me with.' He saw the looks of disbelief on their faces. 'Well, I'll tell you then – but you must swear never to tell, for they wouldn't like it if they knew I told anyone.' He waited until they had all promised, and then he whispered. 'They pay me with magic powers!'

'What sort of magic powers?' one of the men asked, curious now.

Rory looked across the waves towards the island. The sun was sinking down behind it and the water was shining red-gold. If you looked quickly at the island at this time of day, it was easy to imagine that it might be a fairy palace in disguise.

'What sort of magic powers?' the man asked again.

Rory looked at him. 'I really shouldn't say. . .'

'But we've promised,' the man said.

'Oh, all right then,' he said. 'They've given me *knowledge*.'

'*Knowledge?* What sort of knowledge?'

Rory Dearg shrugged. 'All sorts of knowledge. I can never be tricked now, because I'll be able to see through the trick. No one can ever lie to me, because I'll know it's a lie. Why, I even know the fairies' secrets!' He stuck his hands in his pockets and nodded importantly. 'Even they can't trick me!'

And that was a lie.

And what Rory Dearg didn't know was at that very moment, two of the tiny fairy folk were hiding in a small hollow in the ground under a broad flat stone just behind him.

The small group of friends and neighbours broke up as night fell and the first stars began to sparkle in the sky. Rory Dearg climbed up the little twisting path that led to his cottage. From the distance he could see the lights in the windows and he saw a shadow moving across them. That would be his wife Moire, preparing supper.

The track led down across two fields and then out onto a small track that led to his door, and Rory was just about to cross the first field when he felt a cold wind ruffle his hair. His skin prickled and his eyes stung with dust, making him squeeze them shut.

And when he opened his eyes again, the field was gone and in its place a broad, foaming river rushed past, heading down towards the sea.

Rory stopped in amazement, his eyes and mouth open wide. What had happened? He looked around, but everything else seemed to be all right. He could still see the lights of his own cottage across the field – the river now, he corrected himself.

'How am I going to get home?' he asked aloud.

There was a sudden flapping of wings and Rory was shaken by a gust of wind. He looked up... just as a golden eagle folded its wings and dropped to the ground beside him. The bird was huge, far bigger than any eagle Rory had ever seen. Its plumage was a rich golden colour, shot through with bronze and copper feathers. Its claws were as thick as Rory's arm, and the bird was so heavy that they sank slightly into the earth. Its great black eyes blinked slowly as they stared at the frightened man. Suddenly it opened its beak and Rory jumped.

'I can help you,' it said, in a deep rich voice.

Rory could only stare in astonishment at the creature. He opened his mouth to say something, but nothing came out.

'I won't harm you.' The huge eagle took a step closer and raised his head until its eyes were almost on a level with Rory's.

The man tried to speak again, and he eventually said, 'You

can speak!'

The eagle laughed, a deep, chuffing sound. 'Of course I can talk. All creatures can speak – but not all humans can hear them speak.'

Rory took a deep breath. 'What has happened to the field?' he said at last.

The golden eagle's wings shook. 'Fairy work that!' he said. 'You must have offended them somehow.'

'But I haven't done anything to them,' Rory protested.

The huge black eyes seemed to grow. 'But have you said something about them, or spoken about them, or even told a lie about them?' The creature chuffed in laughter again. 'They don't like people telling lies about them.'

Rory Dearg suddenly remembered the stories he had told a little earlier. He felt his broad face burning with shame. He stuck his hands in his pockets and shuffled his feet. 'Well. . .' he began.

'Well?' the eagle said.

'Perhaps I did,' he said at last.

The giant eagle nodded. 'Perhaps you did.'

Rory looked across the river towards his home, and then looked back at the eagle. 'Could you help me?' he asked.

'That's why I'm here,' the eagle said. 'Climb up onto my back and I'll carry you across.'

Rory looked at the huge eagle and hesitated. He had often heard stories about eagles – and golden eagles especially – carrying human children off to their nests. This eagle was so big he could easily carry a fully grown man. He looked at the fast-flowing river again. 'I might be able to swim,' he said doubtfully.

The eagle chuffed again. 'You would be swept away to the sea.'

Rory nodded. 'I suppose you're right.' He walked around behind the huge bird and, taking a fistful of gleaming feathers, he hoisted himself up onto its broad back and settled behind the wings.

'Are you ready now?' the eagle asked.

Rory felt his heart begin to pound hard against his chest. 'I'm ready,' he said in a high-pitched squeak.

The eagle spread his wings and the man felt the bird's body tense and then with two powerful flaps, the bird seemed to leap straight up into the air. Rory shouted and gripped the eagle's feathers all the more tightly as the earth just fell away beneath him. He squeezed his eyes shut.

Rory Dearg opened his eyes again when the huge bird stopped moving. He expected to see his own small white-washed cottage, with its two lighted windows and a curl of white smoke rising from the chimney – but what he did see was a barren, rocky mountainside, with nothing but grey stone covered with grey dust stretching in all directions. Above the mountain the sky was a purple-black colour and the stars were hard and sharp and brilliant.

With a heave of its shoulder muscles, the eagle threw him off. Rory landed with a thump in the soft grey dust. It rose up in a slow, swirling cloud and then gently fell around him, covering him in grey. He looked up at the eagle in astonishment. 'Where have you brought me – and why?'

The eagle laughed its chuffing laugh. 'The fairies asked me to do them a favour,' he said. 'You shouldn't have told that lie about them.' The bird turned its great head and looked at the desolate landscape. 'These are the Mountains of the Moon,' he said.

'But how am I going to get home?' Rory cried.

The eagle shrugged. 'I don't know.' It pointed with one of its massive wings. 'Don't go over there though,' it said, 'otherwise you might just fall off this world.' It paused and then added, with a chuff, 'It's flat, you see.' The golden bird chuffed again, and then rose up on its powerful wings, causing the grey dust to rise and billow – and when the dust had cleared, the bird had gone.

Rory sat on the ground and held his head. He felt like screaming and shouting and crying, but, after a while, he got up and made his way across the dusty ground towards a series of low jagged hills, to the spot where the eagle had told him not to go.

He stopped when he reached them and looked down in amazement. There was nothing beyond the hills. The ground dropped down, down, down... like a cliff. And he couldn't see the bottom.

He heard a noise behind him and spun around. There was no one there, but even as he watched, the dust began to shift and rise, and then a square door in the side of one of the low hills opened and a small, grey-skinned, grey-haired and grey-eyed man came out. He was wearing a long grey robe and carrying a tall stick of grey wood.

'Go away,' he said, in a dry cracked voice.

'But...' Rory began.

'I don't want to listen to any excuses,' the grey man said. 'Go away.'

'Where do I go?' Rory managed to say at last.

'I don't know,' the grey man said, 'but just go away.'

'Well, you'll have to help me,' Rory said firmly.

The grey man smiled a grey smile. 'I'll help you,' he said and took a step nearer Rory. 'Go away,' he suddenly said, and struck him in the chest with his stick.

Rory toppled backwards, his arms twirling, and then the edge of the cliff crumbled away and he sailed out off the edge of the Moutains of the Moon – and fell.

'And don't lie about the fairies again,' the grey man called after him.

Rory fell and fell and fell and fell, down, down, down and down. He saw the stars go flashing by, and then this huge blue-white ball came at him. He tried to duck – but suddenly he was inside the ball and still falling. It was hot and then cold, dry and then wet as he went through a fluffy-white cloud – and then he realised that he was falling back to earth!

Rory saw many shapes moving beneath him, forming one long V shape. He was just beginning to wonder what it was when he crashed into it. It was a flock of geese.

'Help!' he shouted.

'Why?' a bubbly voice asked.

'Because I'm falling,' he screamed.

'Then you shouldn't have jumped,' the same bubbly voice said, but something caught the neck of his shirt and he hung, arms and legs dangling and the ground far, far below.

Rory looked up into the long flat head of a wild goose. Its heavy black beak was holding onto the neck of his shirt. 'I didn't jump,' he said at last, and then he told the goose what had happened.

The kindly creature nodded, and said in its muffled, bubbly voice (because it couldn't open its beak), 'The fairies don't like to be lied about. This is their way of getting their own back.'

'Help me to get home please,' Rory said, 'and I promise that there will be a place for every goose and gander in the pond at the end of my field. And I'll never tell another lie about the *Sidhe*.'

The goose nodded. 'Well, I'll do the best I can, but you're a long way from home. I might not be able to carry you all the way back.'

However, the goose flew on, its wings beating slowly and powerfully on the cold air. They flew through clouds that were thin and cold, and others that were warm and dry. Sometimes they even flew above the clouds, so that, looking down, they seemed like fluffy balls of wool.

At last the goose said to Rory, 'I can't hold on to you any longer. I'll have to let you go here, but you're above water and not too far from the land of Erin.'

'You can't let me go!' Rory shouted, but it was too late. He fell again, down, down, and down. He fell through a cloud and just had time to shout with surprise when he saw something blue and white come rushing up to meet him – and he splashed into the sea. He seemed to be going down for ages, when he struck something that was both warm and solid. The thump jarred every bone in his body, and he held on with all his might as the ground began to move up towards the surface.

When it broke through the waves, he found he was lying

on the back of a huge whale. Its tiny black eyes looked back at him, and, Rory thought, if a whale were able to have an expression on its face, this one would have looked annoyed.

'Eating I was, having a snack,' the whale boomed suddenly, 'minding my own business, not even chasing the fishes, when what happens, you come crashing into me. . .'

'I'm sorry,' Rory said, 'I didn't mean. . .'

'Oh, I know. I'll bet you didn't mean to tell lies about the fairies, but you did. Well, don't think we don't know about it.' The whale paused and seemed to take a deep breath. 'Now, get off my back!'

'I can't,' Rory said, 'I can't swim.'

'Of course you can,' the whale boomed, 'everyone can swim.'

'But I can't,' Rory said again. 'I never learnt!'

'Well, it's about time you did then,' the whale said – and spouted. A thin gush of water suddenly shot out of the blow-hole on the top of his head. It caught Rory in the seat of his trousers and pushed him up into the air. He closed his eyes feeling the rush of wind past his face. . .

And when he opened them again, he was lying on his back on the beach with his wife standing over him with an empty bucket in one hand and a towel in the other which she was shaking in his face.

Rory told his wife the story, and he told many of his friends and neighbours the same story over the next few days – but no one believed him. They all said that he must have fallen asleep on the beach and dreamt it all.

Rory himself might have agreed with them – except for two strange things: the grey dust in his pockets and the golden eagle's feather that was stuck in his coat!

The Fairy Dance

Time is different in fairy land: what may seem to be only hours there might be years in this world. This is a story about a young girl who went into that magical land.

Paul sat up in bed suddenly. He could hear music coming from outside. He knew it was late because the house was very, very quiet, and the moonbeam, which had slanted in through his window when he went to bed, was now around over the other side of the room.

He got out of bed and tiptoed over to the window and peered out. The full moon lit up everything in a ghostly silver-white light, and somehow made the shadows seem even darker.

But he could see no one.

He listened hard, trying to fix the direction of the sound. It was a thin, high sound, much like that of a pipe or flute, or perhaps even the delicate sound of a harp – and it seemed to be coming from the little clump of trees that lay at the bottom of the field.

Paul suddenly shivered, not with the cold but with excitement. He crept back to his bed and began pulling on his shirt and trousers, grabbing his cardigan as he slipped from the room.

In the next room, his sister Brona tossed and turned in her sleep. She was dreaming about a waterfall and the musical sound it made as it splashed into the pool beneath. And then she dreamt that she was standing on a plank of wood that was being tossed around on a stormy sea. Suddenly the wood tilted and she fell off – and woke up. Her brother Paul was shaking her.

'Wake up, wake up,' he whispered.

'What's wrong?' she mumbled, wondering what time it was.

'Music,' he said excitedly. 'I can hear music from outside.'

'What time is it?' she demanded, coming more awake, and realising how dark the room was.

'Oh, it's very late. Everyone's gone to bed, and the moon is beginning to sink.'

'It must be three in the morning,' Brona said angrily, pushing herself up into a sitting position. She was a year older than her brother, and liked to consider herself more grown up.

'That doesn't matter,' Paul said. 'Someone is playing music outside,' he said slowly and distinctly.

'At three o'clock in the morning?' Brona said in amazement. 'You're dreaming!'

'Listen,' he said. 'Just listen.'

Brona listened. And she too heard the music.

She hopped out of bed and together she and Paul stood on either side of the window peering out from behind the curtains. 'I think it's coming from over there,' Paul said, pointing down towards the trees.

His sister nodded. 'I think so too.'

'Let's go and look,' Paul said.

'But the time...' his sister began.

'Tomorrow's Saturday – we don't have to be up for school, and no one will know. We'll just creep out by the back door and have a look. It might be a gypsy caravan,' he added excitedly.

'Or the Fairy Host,' Brona whispered.

'Fairy Host!' Paul laughed quietly. He didn't believe in fairies. He wasn't too sure about ghosts, though.

Brother and sister crept down the garden path, keeping in close to the bushes and making for the wooden gate. The music was louder now, and once they thought they heard the distant sounds of voices and laughter.

They slipped through the gate and headed down the path

towards the sounds of the music. It was louder and clearer now, and the voices were much clearer also. Paul and Brona stopped and listened. The language was not English and although it sounded something like Irish, they weren't able to make out what was being said.

'I think it's gypsies,' Paul said, 'and that must be their secret language, *Shelta.*'

Brona shook her head. 'I don't think so,' she whispered. 'It sounds... almost familiar.' She looked over at her brother, her eyes shining silver in the moonlight. 'It's almost as if we should know it,' she said.

Paul nodded. There was something about the language...

They crept through the bushes and down along the banks of a tiny stream that ran past the foot of their garden. There were three broad, flat stones that they used as stepping stones, and once over these they were into the fringes of the little forest. Long thin beams of moonlight slanted in through the branches of the trees, speckling the ground with patches of deep shadow, making it almost impossible for them to see where they were going.

Suddenly Brona laid her hand on Paul's arm. He jumped and bit his lip in fright.

'What's that?' she whispered, and he could just make out the shape of her arm pointing straight ahead.

Paul squinted in the direction she was pointing. For a moment he could see nothing, and then he saw a light – more of a dim glow really – between the trees. A cloud slid across the face of the moon, and the little forest went absolutely black, and they suddenly found that they could see the glow all the more clearly, and, at the same time, the sound of the music and laughter seemed to increase.

Holding each other's hands they crept towards the glow.

There was a sudden blare of trumpets, and everything lit up like a firework, with streamers of coloured light darting and slipping through the trees and into the heavens. There were red and green and blue sparks cartwheeling and spinning along the forest floor, and ribbons of what looked like fire – although they didn't seem to burn – snaked along the little pathways.

The young boy and girl were suddenly very frightened. Paul tugged on his sister's hand. 'Come on – let's go,' he hissed.

She shook her head and pulled her hand free. 'No – listen!'

'I can't hear anything...' he began, but she squeezed his hand tight, and he shut up. He listened again, and then he heard it, faint and distant but becoming clearer – the brittle sound of horses' hooves. They crouched down into the bushes and huddled together.

There was a flash of movement down along the path and then the bushes parted and two creatures marched into the little clearing. They were small, stout men, dressed in bright red waistcoats, with long heavy green coats over them. They wore old fashioned three-cornered hats, green tights, and beautifully made shoes with huge silver buckles on their feet.

'Leprechauns!' Brona whispered in astonishment.

The two leprechauns held back the bushes as a dozen tiny winged creatures hurried past them and then fluttered up into the low branches of the trees that lined the path.

And then the horses and their riders came into the clearing.

There were two of them. Both horses were tall and thin, with sharp angular features and long pointed ears. Their eyes were huge and glowed brightly, and were slit-pupilled, like a cat's.

Their riders were equally strange. The man was very tall, with a sharp, pointed face and snow-white hair. His clothes were old-fashioned, but beautifully made and of the best fabrics, and there was a sword with a blade of what looked like glass tied to his high saddle.

He was followed by a woman; a small, delicate woman who looked no older than Brona – except for her eyes, which were very old indeed. Her cheek-bones were high and her eyes almost slanted. Her hair was silver-white and flowed down her back in a long shimmering wave. Like the man, she was dressed in the fashion of another age, in a long, trailing gown of green silk, that was decorated along the hem and about the neck and sleeves with a ancient Celtic design.

'Who. . . who are they?' Paul whispered into his sister's ear.

'They are the Shining Folk, the *Sidhe,* the Tuatha De Danann,' Brona murmured, almost as much to herself as to her brother.

'Fairies?'

Brona nodded. 'Fairies. That must be their king and queen.'

'But what are they doing here?' Paul asked.

His sister shrugged. 'I don't know. It must be one of their gatherings, when all the fairy folk come together to sing and dance through the night. You now,' Brona insisted, 'you often see the rings of pale grass in the mornings, or circles of mushrooms that have sprung up overnight.'

Paul nodded. 'I've seen them.'

The lord and lady of the *Sidhe* rode slowly past the bushes which hid the boy and girl, although Brona thought she saw the lady glance down as she passed and smile at their hiding place. The two leprechauns hurried past and once again held back the bushes to allow them to ride into the wide glowing circle.

Paul and Brona caught a glimpse of the gathering before the leprechauns stepped through and allowed the bushes to drop back. In that instant they had seen a huge gathering of creatures and beings from Ireland's mythology: there were not only leprechauns, but cluricauns, fir dearg, fir bolg, and tall, wild-haired women with sorrowful eyes, that they guessed must be the dreaded banshee. There were animals also, huge dogs, long-horned cows, bright-eyed hares and rabbits and a wild-maned, savage-looking horse, that they knew must be the terrible Phooka, the demon-horse.

When the bushes closed on the scene, the music began once again – a thin, high, very delicate sound. Other musical instruments joined in and soon the tiny forest was alive with sound.

Paul tugged on his sister's arm. 'Come on, let's go.'

'Not yet. Let's get closer.'

Paul shook his head. 'Don't be silly. We're lucky they didn't spot us when they rode past. What do you think would happen if they caught us?'

Someone began to sing in the clearing, and the shouting and laughter died down as the haunting voice drifted out over the land. It was so beautiful that Brona shivered with the sound of it.

'Brona... please,' Paul asked, 'can we go?'

'I wonder who's singing,' his sister said softly. 'I'll bet it's the fairy queen...' She got up on her hands and knees and began to creep towards the clearing.

'Brona, don't!' Paul hissed, but she just ignored him and continued crawling towards the light and sound.

She was nearly there when the song finished and the Fairy Host cried aloud in its strange language, applauding the singer. Then someone began to beat a drum, and an instrument that sounded like bagpipes started up, and then trumpets joined in and soon the whole company was singing and swirling around to the dance music.

Paul felt his heart begin to pound in time to the music and he pressed his hands to his ears to try and shut out the sounds. But he could still feel the music throbbing up through the ground.

It made him want to dance...

Brona! He looked for his sister. He could just about make out her shape outlined against the bushes ahead of him. She was swaying in time to the music and even as he looked she began to part the bushes that hid her from the Fairy Host...

'No!' he shouted, but he couldn't be heard above the throbbing of the music. He scrambled forward, but he was too late. Brona had joined in the fairy dance.

And then the whole clearing lit up with a ghostly coloured fire, and he fell back covering his stinging eyes. When he could see again, the Fairy Host, and his sister were gone.

There was a big search for Brona, but she was never found.

No one believed Paul's story. He had been dreaming, they said, and eventually his family moved away from the village and settled in Dublin where the fairy folk were spoken of only with a smile. Paul grew up and moved away from Ireland, travelling all over the world, but always promising to return to the village of his childhood.

The old white-haired man made his way down the track that led to the stream. In sixty years it hadn't changed much – except that it seemed much smaller now than it had once seemed to a nine-year-old boy. He stopped and looked back; the house was still there, of course. It was boarded up now, with slates missing from the roof and paint peeling off the walls. But it was more or less as he remembered it. He turned his back on it and continued on down towards the stream.

The old man paused by the edge of the little stream. Had it really shrunk, or had it just seemed much wider when he was a boy? The stepping stones were still there, and he crossed quickly to the far side. The forest hadn't changed at all. It still looked as dark and forbidding as it always had.

He shrugged and followed the winding animal track that led through the trees. The afternoon was very quiet and warm and he loosened his collar. He was glad he hadn't brought an umbrella. Once he stepped away from the stream the sound of water disappeared and he could only hear the distant trilling of a thrush.

And then it stopped and the afternoon was silent.

He heard the strange sound then. He stopped and listened, tilting his head from side to side and squinting into the bushes. He had just about decided that it was probably the sound of the water behind him when he heard it again – it was the sound of a child crying.

The old man pushed his way through the bushes and came out into a clearing – and found himself facing a young girl. She had her head buried in her hands and was crying bitterly – but he would have recognised the bright red hair anywhere.

'Brona?' he whispered.

The girl jumped with fright. When she looked up, her face was blotchy from crying and her eyes were red and swollen. 'Who are you?' she sniffed.

'Brona!' he said, 'it's you!'

'Yes, I'm Brona. Who are you?' the young girl asked. She looked hard at the old man. 'You look familiar, but I don't think I've ever seen you before.'

'We met a long time ago,' the old man whispered.

'When?' Brona demanded. 'I don't think I've met you.' She stood up and brushed grass and straw off her dress. 'And now I really must be getting home, my mother and father will be getting worried.'

The old man shook his head. 'They're not looking for you,' he said softly. She opened her mouth to ask a question, but he held up his hand. 'What do you last remember?' he asked softly.

'I remember the Fairy Host, and dancing, dancing, dancing with them. My brother wouldn't dance with them though, but I danced the whole night through with them.'

'Brona,' the old man said gently, 'I am your brother Paul, you've been away with the fairies for more than sixty years!'

Brona lived with her brother Paul for many years afterwards. They moved away to Dublin where everyone thought that they were uncle and niece. Brona later became a famous dancer for she danced, and even walked, with beautiful grace and poise.

There is a country saying that anyone who has danced with the fairies, will hear their music forever after.

The Wise Woman's Payment

It is not wise to make an enemy of one of the Little Folk, because they can be very cruel and spiteful when they are annoyed. However, a leprechaun can be a very good friend to have. They are usually kind and considerate, and are always full of good advice.

Nano Hayes was a wise woman, a mná allthacha. She knew all the herbs that could cure, and she was even able to see into the future. If she made a cure from her huge stock of herbs, she only charged a few pence, and if the people hadn't got the money with them she would tell them to drop it in when they were passing her cottage. Sometimes they forgot, and she was too kind-hearted to ask for it directly. And then there were other people, who just didn't bother paying at any time.

But she did manage to get payment of a sort in the end. . .

The old woman sat down on the hard, wooden chair and rested her elbows on the scratched wooden table. She looked at the small jar that sat on the table in front of her. 'That's all I have left,' she said, looking across towards the fireplace.

The small, dark man sitting there put down the shoe he was mending and stuck his needle in the collar of his coat. He was called Seamus Bán and he was a leprechaun, a fairy shoemaker. 'What's all you have left?' he asked.

Nano Hayes picked up the small jar and shook it. Something rustled dryly inside. 'This is the last jar of healing herbs I have left,' she said.

'Where did the rest go to?' Seamus asked, his lined face crinkling up into a frown.

'Well, I've used them all,' Nano Hayes said. She was a small, frail woman, with a round, wrinkled face, and thick grey hair that matched the colour of her eyes. 'I used a lot last month when nearly everyone in the village caught that bad cold, and then there was that rash that the boys in the school got when they fell into those nettles...'

'How did you cure that?' Seamus asked. Leprechauns, because they were so small, were often stung by nettles.

'Well, I rubbed a fresh dock leaf on the sting,' Nano Hayes said, 'they're very good. But you can also bathe the sting with vinegar, especially apple-cider vinegar – and that's also very good for those blisters you get from poison ivy.'

'Now isn't that a strange thing,' Seamus Bán said, 'the Little Folk can handle poison ivy with no bad effects – although I know humans never should.'

'We must have different types of skin,' Nano Hayes said. She got up and went to the big cupboard on the wall. She picked up another jar and shook it. 'I've no walnuts either,' she said.

'What do you want walnuts for?' the leprechaun asked.

'The girls in the village often come to me looking for something to clear their skins and make their eyes bright and sparkling. Walnuts are very good for a clear skin.' She continued searching through the cupboard, shaking jars and putting them to one side. 'You boil about fifteen or twenty large walnuts in water, until the water starts to look dirty, and then you wash your face in the water.'

Seamus smiled. 'And what happens when you wash your face in this dirty water?' he asked rubbing his own dirty face.

Nano Hayes laughed, 'It's not dirty water. It's only the oils from the walnuts. It will clear up your skin in days. But if you don't like that, you can always use half an apple, cucumber or a potato and rub them in against your skin.'

'The Little People always wash their faces in the first dew of a May morning, just before the sun rises,' the leprechaun said.

Nano Hayes nodded. 'Yes, humans can do that also.' She stepped back and closed the doors of her cupboard gently.

In her hand she held another small jar.

'What's in that?' Seamus asked.

'Mint,' she said.

'We make a sort of tea out of mint,' he said.

'So do we,' the woman said. She crossed the room to the table and sat down again.

Seamus got up from his chair by the fire and sat down opposite her. 'Where have all the herbs gone?' he asked. 'Why haven't you bought more?'

'I've used them all,' she said, 'and no one has paid me for them yet. I can't buy any more because I've no money.' She shook her head. 'Anyway, I usually pick my own herbs fresh from the mountain and river sides; I only buy those you cannot find around here.'

Seamus looked thoughtful. 'So, why can't you go out and pick them yourself?' he asked.

Nano Hayes shrugged again. 'Because I need so many – and because winter will soon be here and a lot of my herbs will be dead by then. I really must have them picked by the day after tomorrow at the latest.'

'Will the villagers not help you?' Seamus asked.

The old woman shook her head. 'I don't want to ask them.'

'But they ask you when they need help.'

'That's different,' Nano Hayes said.

'No, it's not.'

'Well, I'm not going to ask them to spend all day picking herbs, grasses, leaves and berries just for me,' she protested.

'Tell them it's your payment for all the cures they haven't paid for,' the leprechaun said.

'I couldn't do that,' she said in amazement.

'Well pay them then,' the small man said, smiling hugely.

'With what?' Nano Hayes asked, 'I've no money to buy herbs, so how can I offer to pay them?'

Seamus Bán smiled again, his wide grin almost splitting his face in two. He slipped off the chair and went back over to the fire, where he rummaged about in his brown cloth bag, which he carried everywhere.

'What are you doing?' the old wise woman asked.

'Looking.'

'Looking for what?'

'For this!' The leprechaun stood up with a heavy-looking brown bundle in his hand. He shook it and it gave a muffled clink.

Nano Hayes suddenly looked doubtful. 'If that's what I think it is. . .' she began.

Seamus climbed back up into the chair and placed the heavy bundle down on the wooden table. 'And what do you think it is?' he asked.

'I think it's leprechaun gold,' she said.

Seamus Bán laughed in his jolly voice. 'So that's why they call you a wise woman,' he said, opening the knot that held the bundle together, and pulling the cloth apart. A rich, warm golden-yellow glow lit up the dark room, for on the table were a hundred large golden coins.

Nano Hayes' mouth opened into a big 'O' of surprise. She had never seen so much money before in all her years. She touched it carefully with a finger, not sure whether it was real or not. But it chinked together like real money.

'You can have it,' Seamus Bán said.

The old woman looked shocked. 'I will not!'

But the leprechaun nodded insistently. 'Yes, you will. You've been good to the Little Folk, Nano, and you've never accepted anything for your help. Well, now we can help you – and you cannot refuse our help.'

'But it's such a lot of money,' the old woman said.

'But it's fairy gold,' Seamus Bán said, and winked.

And then the old woman understood and she smiled broadly. She picked up the four ends of the cloth and tied the money up in a neat bundle, and slipped it into her apron pocket.

That same afternoon, Nano Hayes walked into the village and told everyone she met that if they were to come up to her house at dawn the following morning, they would have a chance of making some money. Soon the whole village knew, and everyone was very curious to know how they were going to earn this money. But Nano Hayes would say nothing, only tell them to be outside her door at dawn.

The next morning there was a huge crowd outside Nano Hayes' cottage. The sky to the east was bright with the coming dawn, although overhead the stars still sparkled, and sunrise was still a little way away. Nearly everyone from the village was there, and the morning air was filled with a low buzz as they talked quietly amongst themselves, wondering why the old wise woman had brought them out so early.

A cock crowed on the cottage's thatched roof and the door opened. Nano Hayes walked out into the cold morning air. She was carrying a heavy-looking bundle that chinked and clinked as she walked.

'I would like to thank you all for coming here,' she said. 'I am pleased to see I have so many friends in the village.' She paused and looked at the faces. Most of them were looking at the bundle she held in her hand, wondering what it held.

'In the past few months,' she continued, 'I have used up all my healing herbs, and now, with winter fast approaching, I find I am very short. So I have asked you here today to help me pick the herbs, leaves, bark, berries, roots and weeds that I will need to make my cures.'

The crowd looked puzzled and some murmured angrily. This was not what they had expected.

'Of course,' Nano Hayes continued, 'I don't expect you to do this for nothing, and everyone who helps me will receive one gold piece.' She dipped her hand into the bundle and pulled out one shining gold coin and held it up.

The crowd murmured like a swarm of bees.

'Are there any questions?' she asked, putting the coin back into the bundle, where everyone heard it clink against the others.

'Yes,' someone in the crowd said. 'Where did you get all that money?'

Nano Hayes smiled widely. 'It's fairy gold,' she said.

So for the rest of the day, the people of the village wandered up the hills and through the little valleys, looking for the herbs and roots for Nano Hayes. They looked for the bark of certain trees, and the berries from different bushes, they picked dandelions and mushrooms, and some even wandered down onto the beach to pick up seaweed for her.

Soon, a huge bundle of bits and pieces began to gather outside the wise woman's door, where she sat on a low, three-legged stool sorting everything out. By early afternoon, she had everything she needed for another year, but still it continued coming and by evening, when the sun was beginning to sink into the west, she had enough to last her for the next two years.

As the villagers began to trickle in, hot and tired, some scratched and bruised, Nano Hayes gave each of them a single gold coin, saying, 'Now, remember, this is fairy gold,' and then she would add, 'Do you owe anyone any money?'

Now a few people thought about it, and then they smiled shyly and handed the money back to the old woman, saying, 'That's for the medicine you made me a while ago.' But to these Nano Hayes would shake her head and press the coin back into their hand, and tell them that they had worked hard enough for their money.

But others would just look her straight in the eye and shake their heads and say that they owed no one any money.

By the time the first stars began to twinkle in the night sky, the last of the villagers had gone to their homes and the bag of money was empty. Nano Hayes and Seamus Bán stood by the door of her cottage and looked down at the lights of the village.

'Well now, wasn't that a good idea of mine?' the leprechaun asked, looking at the tied up bundles of herbs and grasses.

The old woman nodded. 'It certainly was. But it cost you a lot of money,' she said.

The small man shook his head and laughed. 'Not as much as you might think,' he said. 'Don't forget, that was fairy money you gave them.'

And then he and Nano Hayes went back inside, laughing.

Fairy money is a strange thing. The next morning, those people who had lied and said that they owed nothing, found that their fairy money had turned to a lump of stone.

The Shoemaker and Himself

This is a story about a shoemaker who made a promise to a stranger who turned out to be none other than the devil himself.

Sean Lane had always been a strange man, and from the moment he was born, people said that there was something amiss with him. He was small and dark with a sharp, pointed face and hard bright eyes. When he was a young boy, he would often stop and stare at something only he could see and then he would turn to his brother or sister and say, 'Did you not see the leprechaun?' or 'That was one of the fairy folk.'

Of course, no one believed him. They all thought he was just a strange little boy, who used to tell lies.

But the truth was that Sean could actually see the fairy folk – the *Sidhe,* and the leprechauns and cluricauns and fir dearg and once he even saw the terrible banshee singing her terrifying lament outside a house to warn them of death.

When he grew up, Sean decided he would be a shoemaker. His own grandfather was a cobbler and would be able to teach him how to make and mend shoes and Sean – who was something of a lazy person – thought that cobbling would be an easy sort of job. On summer days he would be able to sit outside his cottage, mending the shoes, and in winter he would be able to sit in front of a roaring fire. So, Sean went and lived with his grandfather for three years learning how to become a shoemaker, and in the end, when he thought he knew enough, he said good-bye to the old man and returned to his own village.

However, on his way home, Sean decided to take a short

cut across the marsh. It was a dark and dreary place even on the hottest and brightest day, and the young shoemaker soon regretted his decision. The ground bubbled and steamed and swarms of flies and midges buzzed around his head. Once, he stumbled off the narrow path and sank ankle-deep into the thick, dirty water. He got such a fright that he decided to sit down and rest for a while before continuing across the marsh.

But the day was a hot one, and Sean soon fell asleep with his head resting against an ancient tree-stump. He awoke much later with a start, shivering with the evening chill. It took him a moment to realise where he was and then he wondered what had awakened him. He lay still and listened.

For a moment he heard nothing unusual, but then, faint and almost lost in the buzzing and sucking and creaking noises of the marsh, he heard a thin metallic plinking sound. Sean sat up and listened carefully. The noise sounded very familiar. He turned his head slightly towards the sound – and then he suddenly recognised it. It was the sound of a shoemaker's hammer hitting a nail.

But what would a shoemaker be doing in this part of the marsh?

The noise was coming from ahead of him, and Sean made up his mind to investigate. On hands and knees he crept down the path, heading towards the sound. The ringing noises grew louder as he neared it, and then Sean smelt the bitter-sweet odour of tobacco on the air. When the sound was coming from directly in front of him, Sean carefully raised his head and parted the thick blades of grass.

He found he was staring directly at a leprechaun. The small man was sitting on a little mound of earth beneath the shade of a weeping willow tree, and Sean could see the black three-cornered hat, the dark green coat and the corners of his bright red stockings.

The young man could feel his heart beginning to pound. He had seen leprechauns a few times before but only from the distance. They were very hard to catch, but if you

managed to get hold of one and not take your eyes off him even for an instant, they would have to lead you to their hidden pots of gold. However, they had a hundred tricks for making sure they cheated you, and there were very many stories about the Little People escaping from the Big Folk – which was what they called humans. But this one would not get away, Sean promised. He took a deep breath and began to slide forward on the damp ground.

The leprechaun should have heard the young man approaching, but it was a very hot day and he was tired and so he wasn't really paying attention to his surroundings. He heard nothing because he was tapping the shoe in his hand with his hammer and humming a little tune. So, he got a terrible fright when someone grabbed him by the shoulders and shouted, 'I've got you now, Mr Leprechaun, and you won't cheat me!'

The leprechaun turned around and looked up at the Big Person. The Big Person, the leprechaun decided, really wasn't such a big person after all; indeed, he was only a little bigger than himself.

Sean looked at the leprechaun. Although he had the face and beard of an old man, his eyes were bright and lively, and he didn't really seem to be too worried about being caught.

'I've got you now,' Sean said, still holding the leprechaun by the shoulders of his green coat.

'Aye, you have indeed,' the leprechaun said quietly.

'I won't let you go.'

The leprechaun shook his head. 'No, I didn't think you would. Now, tell me, what do you want from me?'

Sean was a little surprised. Why wasn't the leprechaun frightened or angry at being captured?

'I suppose you want my crock of gold,' the leprechaun continued, 'well it won't work, because I haven't got one. I was captured last week by one of your people and I had to give up my gold then. And the leprechaun can only have one pot of gold in a lifetime.'

'How do I know you're telling me the truth?' Sean demanded.

'Ah sure, why would I lie to you? The Little People never lie,' he said. 'They may not always tell the full truth, but they'll never tell you a lie.'

'Oh. So you've no gold?' the young man asked.

'Not so much as a gold button,' the leprechaun said pleasantly.

'Nothing?' Sean asked. He was very disappointed; it was just his luck to get hold of a leprechaun that someone else had caught before.

'Not so much as a silver sixpence.'

'Nothing?' he asked again.

'Not so much as a copper penny.'

'Well what do you have?' Sean demanded. 'I can't just let you go now, can I?'

lted his head to one side and considered.

pose you can. It wouldn't really be right if

e go. Why, what would the other Little Folk

iew that I was caught and then just let go. No,'

m, 'I'll either have to escape or pay you.'

u won't escape,' Sean said. 'You see, I've a little of

blood in me, I'm what the country people call fey.

e the *sidhe* and the fairies – so you won't be able to

e that way.'

n well then,' the leprechaun said, 'I'll pay you for my

dom'.

'But if you've neither gold, silver nor copper how can you pay me?'

'With this!' The leprechaun wriggled one hand free and pulled a small leather bag off his shoulder. 'I'll give you this!'

Sean, with one hand still holding tightly onto the Little Folk, took the bag in his free hand. It was a small square leather bag with a strap to go around the shoulder. He opened it, but it was empty inside. However, he didn't refuse the gift just yet. This was a leprechaun's bag and might just be magical.

When he had examined the bag carefully, he asked, 'What's so special about the bag?'

The leprechaun smiled crookedly. 'Well now, I'll tell you. This might just look like a small black bag to you now – but this bag grows! You could put a table and four chairs in here and still have space for more.'

The young man looked at the bag again, and then back to the leprechaun. 'You're sure now?' he said doubtfully.

'Sure I'm sure. And it's a bag that will never wear out or tear,' he added.

'A fine bag altogether,' Sean agreed 'if what you're telling me is the truth.'

'Well, you'll just have to take my word for it,' the leprechaun said.

Sean nodded. 'I suppose I will...' And then he suddenly shook open the bag and popped it over the leprechaun's

head. Now the bag was so small that it should only
covered his head, but it grew...and grew...until the s
man was completely inside it.

'Do you believe me now?' the leprechaun asked in
muffled voice.

Sean stood back and looked at the bag with its wrigglin
contents. It would be very handy to have a bag like that, he
thought. He knelt down and unsnapped the little catches and
shook the leprechaun out. 'I believe you,' he said. 'I'll take
the bag in exchange for your freedom.'

The little man stood up and dusted off his clothes and
straightened his cap on his head. 'Aye, it's a good bag. You
better be off now,' he said, 'it's getting late and you don't
want to be trapped on the marsh at night.'

Sean looked up into the sky which was already beginning
to darken in the east. The first of the night stars were beginning to peep through. He shivered as a cold breeze whistled
through the lonely trees. 'No,' he agreed, 'what we really need
is someone with a lantern to lead us across these marshes
at night.'

The leprechaun looked at him strangely for a moment.
'Aye, that we do.' He nodded, gave a short little bow, turned
– and was gone!

Sean stood for a moment, wondering if he had been dreaming it all – but he did have the small black bag in his hand
as proof. He slung it over his shoulder, pulled his coat tighter
around his shoulders and set off as quickly as possible for
home.

Now the years passed. Some years were good for Sean, and
he sold and mended a lot of shoes and made enough money
to live well – but others were very bad, and he was forced
to borrow food and money from his friends. Strangely,
because Sean was such a good shoemaker, it helped to keep
him poor. It took a long time for his shoes to wear out or
need mending and so the people didn't have to go to him as
often as they would with an ordinary pair of shoes or boots.

There was one very bad winter when he earned practically nothing. The weather was warm and dry, there was little frost and no snow, and no one needed their boots or shoes mended and so for three whole months he had no work. He began to borrow – just a little at first, but soon more and more. In a very short time he owed a lot of money. And soon those he had borrowed from began to get impatient as Spring was approaching and they needed the money to buy crops and seed. But Sean had no money.

It was a bright, though cold February morning and he was sitting on the step outside his little cottage mending his own shoes when he saw the stranger approaching. He was a tall, thin dark man, dressed in a black overcoat, black trousers, shiny black shoes and a black hat. He was smoking a thin black cigar, and the smell of the tobacco was sharp and bitter on the fresh morning air. The stranger stopped at the gate.

'I'm looking for Sean Lane,' he said pleasantly. He spoke Irish with a strange foreign accent, and as he leaned across the gatepost, Sean noticed that he wore black gloves, but with a thick gold ring outside the glove on his little finger.

'I am Sean Lane,' the cobbler said, nodding courteously. 'What can I do for you, sir?'

The stranger smiled and pushed open the gate. 'Ah, but it's not what you can do for me, it's what I can do for you,' he said. He had a thin sort of smile which curled his lips but didn't brighten his eyes.

'I'm not sure I understand you,' Sean said.

The stranger stood before the shoemaker with his hands held behind his back. He was very tall and Sean had to lean back to look up at him. 'It has come to my notice that you are...' he paused, and smiled again. 'Well, it seems you are a little short of money at present...'

'Ach no,' Sean said quickly, beginning to get nervous now, 'I owe a few pounds here and there, that's all. But business is picking up, I'll soon be able to pay it all back.' He stood up. 'You know my name, sir but I'm not sure that you told me yours.'

'I didn't,' the stranger said. 'But some people call me Himself.'

'Himself?'

'Yes,' the tall man smiled again. 'Have you never heard people say, "... it's himself that's coming now..." or "... it was himself did this..."?'

Sean nodded doubtfully. It was a common phrase used by the country people, but he had never thought that they were talking about a real person.

'Now,' Himself said, 'I've come to make a little bargain with you.'

'What sort of bargain?' Sean asked quickly.

'A small sort of one.'

'What are you offering me?'

'I'm offering you money – a lot of money – and the promise of a lot of business, as much as you can handle. When I'm finished, you'll be the best known shoemaker in all Ireland.'

'And what's it going to cost me?' the shoemaker asked doubtfully.

'Only a promise.'

'What's the promise?'

Himself leaned forward until his face was only a few inches away from Sean's. His eyes looked very red. 'The promise is that you will come with me in seven years time. You won't ask any questions either,' he added.

'Where will I go?'

The stranger raised one long thin finger. 'No questions.'

Sean leaned back against the whitewashed wall of his cottage and thought about it. It was a very tempting offer; a lot a money and as much business as he could handle. He wasn't too sure about the other part of the deal though. And he had just a hint of an idea whom the stranger might be. He looked up at Himself. 'Can I think about this offer of yours?' he asked.

The tall man shook his head. 'This is an offer I make to very few people and I only make it once. I'm afraid you must make up your mind now. I've a train to catch to Dublin shortly.'

Sean came to a decision. 'Right then, I'll do it.'

Himself smiled in a very strange way. 'Excellent.' He reached inside his coat and took out a dark leather wallet. It was bulging with money. He pulled out a wad of notes and handed it to the shoemaker. 'Here you are. And I'll make sure you never want for business,' he added. The stranger then turned up the collar of his coat and settled his hat on his head. 'I'll be off now – but I'll see you in seven years time,' he added, his voice sounding like a warning. He nodded once and, before Sean could say anything else, he turned on his heel and walked away quickly, leaving the shoemaker alone with a handful of money.

The seven years seemed to pass very quickly for Sean Lane. As the stranger had promised, his business increased and he soon became famous as the best shoemaker in all Ireland. He moved from his little cottage to a bigger house and soon took on some apprentices. He even started seeing a girl from the nearby town, and he was just about beginning to think about asking her father for permission to marry her when he realised that the seven years were up.

It was a bitterly cold February morning when the stranger returned. Sean had just hopped out of bed and was splashing cold water on his face when he heard the front door bell ring. He stopped. It was only half-past seven, who could be calling so early in the morning? He crept to his bedroom door, put his ear against it and listened.

Downstairs, one of the young maids hurried to open the door. The shoemaker was the only man in the town who could afford to keep servants. The young girl opened the door and then jumped in fright at the figure who stood on the doorstep.

The tall thin man bowed slightly. 'Is this the Lane household?' he asked, first in Irish and then in English, in a strange, foreign-sounding accent.

'It is, sir,' she answered quietly.

'And is Mr Lane at home?' the man asked with a smile.

'He is, sir,' the maid answered. She stepped back and

allowed the stranger to come into the hall. 'What name shall I give him?' she asked.

The tall foreigner smiled again. 'Oh, just say it's Himself.'

The maid hurried upstairs and tapped gently on the shoemaker's door. 'Sir. .?'

Sean opened the door a crack and peeped out. 'I know,' he whispered. 'Tell him I'll be down in a minute.'

Sean hurried around the room, getting dressed. Seven years had certainly passed very quickly, although he had to admit that everything the stranger had promised had come true. Which meant that the stranger could only be. . . the Devil Himself!

The shoemaker smiled then. He had partially guessed his identity seven years ago, and he had only accepted his deal because he had an idea how he might cheat the Devil. Sean Lane smiled again, picked up his magical leprechaun's bag and opened the door.

Himself was waiting at the bottom of the stairs. In the seven years the stranger hadn't changed in the slightest. He even wore the same clothes he had worn then.

'Your time is up,' he said with a smile, 'you have to come with me now.'

Sean nodded. 'I've been expecting you. My bag is packed, and I've everything here that I'll need.'

'I don't think you'll need anything where you're going,' Himself said with a grin.

'Where I go, my bag goes with me,' Sean insisted.

'What's in the bag then?' the stranger asked.

'Oh, I couldn't tell you. A lot of things.'

'You couldn't fit a lot of things into that bag,' Himself said in a mocking voice.

'It holds enough for me,' the shoemaker said.

'Let me see then.'

'No.'

'But it won't hurt to let me see, now will it?' Himself asked.

'Well. . .' Sean shrugged. 'Oh, I suppose it won't.' He knelt on the bottom step and opened the bag. The stranger knelt down beside him. He peeped into the bag.

'It's empty!' he said.

'It is not,' the shoemaker insisted.

Himself pointed. 'Look for yourself; there's nothing in it.'

'There is,' Sean persisted. 'Look'.

The stranger leaned over and peered closely into the bag – and Sean quickly pulled it up over his head. The bag grew... and grew... and grew... and Sean snapped it shut on the tall thin stranger!

Sean danced a little jig on the bottom step beside the wriggling bag. 'I have you now, and you won't get out until you give back my promise.'

There was a muffled shout from inside the bag, and it sounded like 'No.' Sean heaved the long bag up onto his

shoulder and set off towards the nearby town. The priest there might be able to help him, he thought.

But on his way into town he passed Farmer O'Neill's barn where the farmer and his two sons were threshing corn with flails, which were like small whips.

'A good-morning to you, Mr O'Neill,' he said, stopping by the door, resting his bag on the ground by his feet.

The farmer and his two sons stopped and nodded to the shoemaker. 'You're up early this morning, Mr Lane,' the old farmer said.

'Oh, I think today will be a busy day for me – and for you too, I see,' he said, pointing to the corn.

The farmer nodded, 'Aye, we've a lot to do.' He stopped and pointed to the bag. 'What have you got there, if you don't mind my asking?'

'A bag full of leather,' the shoemaker said, 'but it's very hard and I'm taking it into town to get it softened.'

'And how will you get it softened?' the farmer asked.

'Oh, I'll have it beaten for a while; that'll soften it up.'

'Beaten is it? Well now, if you give it here, the two lads and myself will beat it for you.'

'That's very kind of you,' Sean said, handing the black bag to the farmer.

'Will we take it out of the bag for you?' one of the farmer's son's asked, reaching for the lock.

'No, no,' Sean said quickly. 'If you take the leather out of the bag the. . . flails might mark and tear the surface,' he said, saying the first thing that came into his mind.

Mr O'Neill nodded. 'Of course. Well then, we'll just beat the whole lot – bag and all. Stand back now,' he warned. Then the farmer and his two sons began to beat the bag with all their might. They pounded on it for one full hour and when they were finished the black bag was soft and limp. The old farmer handed it back to the shoemaker. 'There you are, I hope that's a little better.'

'It is indeed,' Sean said with a big grin. 'Thank you very much for all your trouble.' He heaved the bag over his shoulder and, waving the O'Neill's good-bye, continued on down the road towards the town.

A little further on, Sean came to the Tully Brother's Foundry. The three Tully brothers were blacksmiths, and when the shoemaker arrived, they were busy making and shaping horse-shoes.

One was pumping the bellows to blow air into the fire, making the coals glow white-hot, and the other two were using their heavy hammers to twist thin bars of metal into half circles, which would then be shaped into shoes.

They stopped when they saw Sean passing and wished him a good morning.

'A good-morning to you,' Sean said. 'How are those new shoes I made you a while ago?' he asked Gerard, the oldest and largest of the three brothers.

'They fit like a glove,' the huge man said, 'like a glove. Now, remember what I said to you then, if there's anything I can do for you in return...'

'Well,' Sean said, 'there is something...'

'You just name it,' Gerard said, rubbing his hands on his thick leather apron and leaning on his hammer.

'This is a bag full of leather which I'm taking into town to be softened,' Sean said, holding up the black bag, 'but I was wondering if you could just beat on it for a while – just to help soften it up, you know.'

'Will we not tear the bag?' Gerard wondered.

'Not this bag,' Sean promised, 'it's stronger than it looks.'

So the three Tully brothers took it in turns to beat the bag with their hammers. Each one hammered it for an hour and at the end of three hours they were surprised to find it was still in one piece.

'That's a fine bag you have there,' Gerard said to Sean, handing it back to him. 'If you should every think of selling it, come to me.'

'Oh, I couldn't sell this,' Sean said, 'I've had it for years, it's very special.' He thanked the three blacksmiths and then waved good-bye.

It was now close to midmorning and he had one last stop to make before he had a few more words with Himself.

The shoemaker's final stop was at Devaney's Mill on the hill above the town. Old Mr Devaney had been the miller for nearly forty years. He made all the bread for the town and some for the nearby villages, and his mill was the largest and most famous in the county on account of its huge grinding stones.

Sean made his way up the hill and went in through the always-open door into the back of the mill where the flour was ground. The old miller saw him and waved.

'A good-morning to you, Mr Lane, and what brings you up here? Is it freshly-baked, warm bread you're looking for, eh?'

Sean smiled. Devaney's bread was delicous, and his favourite. 'Oh, I'll have some of your bread Mr Devaney, but I've come to ask a favour of you.'

The white-haired old man smiled broadly. 'Ask away.'

The shoemaker held up the black bag. 'Would you put this bag of mine on your mill, and let it turn for a little while?'

'But that will destroy your bag,' the old man protested.

The shoemaker shook his head. 'Oh, no, this is a stronger bag than it looks.'

'Well if you say so...' Mr Devaney said doubtfully. He took the black bag and put it on the wheel and then the huge mill stone came around and crushed it flat against the second stone. The huge stone rumbled away and then came around again and again and again...

An hour later, Mr Devaney gave the bag back to Sean. 'I'm surprised it's not in shreds,' he said.

'I told you it was a special sort of bag.' He thanked the old miller and set off for home, munching on a warm loaf of bread.

When he returned to his own house, he went out to the barn and set the bag on the ground. He leaned close to it and said, 'I'll let you out if our deal is off. Promise.'

There was a long pause and then the Devil said faintly, 'I promise.'

Sean opened the bag and shook Himself out. The Devil looked very battered and bedraggled, and his fine black clothes were covered with white flour. He got to his feet and shook his fist at the shoemaker. 'You're a terrible man. I don't think I would want you as a devil,' he snapped and then he closed his eyes and disappeared in a crack of blue fire.

The shoemaker leaned back and laughed for a long, long time. He had cheated the Devil.

Sean lived to be a very old man, and he was nearly ninety years old before he died. And of course he went straight to Hell – for he had sold his soul to the Devil, even if Himself wouldn't take it! The door to Hell was made from black marble with large silver bolts set into it and a huge silver knocker in the shape of a dragon's head set in the centre of it. Sean took hold of it and knocked loudly.

For a long time nothing happened and then, slowly, very slowly, the door creaked open. There was no one there. 'Yes?' a voice suddenly asked, booming and echoing as if it came from a great distance.

'Well,' Sean said, 'I've just died, and I've ended up here, so I suppose this is where I've got to come.'

A figure stepped into the doorway. It was the tall thin, dark-faced man with sharp eyes. He wasn't dressed all in black this time, but Sean recognised him.

'Ah, it's yourself,' he smiled.

The Devil started and then looked closely at the man standing on the doorstep. 'You!' He stepped back and shook his head. 'You're not coming in here; I remember what you did to me the last time.'

'Well, where will I go then?' Sean asked.

'You can try the Other Place,' the Devil said and, stepping back, he slammed the door shut.

Sean turned his back on Hell and set off along the road of black marble, returning the way he had come. Soon the colour of the road changed to grey and then to white and he soon saw the white marble gate of Heaven in the distance.

It looked very like the gate of Hell, except that this was all white marble and with gold bolts and studs. It had a gold knocker made in the shape of a smiling angel. Sean took hold of the knocker and gently rapped on the door.

The door was opened almost immediately by a tall, thin figure dressed all in white. Sean tried to see over his shoulders, but he couldn't see any signs of wings. 'Well?' the angel asked pleasantly.

'Well,' Sean began, 'I've just died and although I thought I had to go to Hell, Himself won't take me in.'

'Oh,' the angel looked very surprised. 'What's your name, I'll have to check my books.'

'Sean Lane, shoemaker,' he said.

The angel disappeared for a moment and when he returned he was holding a huge leather-bound book with gold clasps on the corners. He opened the book about half-way and ran his long thin finger down the heavy pages. 'Lane... Lane... yes, yes, here we are.' He read a few lines and then looked down at the shoemaker. 'Sold your soul to Himself, did you? Well, we cannot have you here...'

'But he won't have me down there,' Sean protested. 'What am I going to do?'

The angel considered for a moment, and then he read some more of the shoemaker's life. Finally, he looked up and smiled. 'We'll have to send you back,' he said.

'Back?'

'Yes, back down to Earth. We'll give you a penance to do, and maybe in a few hundred years you'll be able to come in here.'

Sean nodded. 'What do I have to do then?'

The angel tapped the page with his finger. 'It says here that you once said that there should be someone with a light to lead people across dangerous marshes at night.

'Did I say that?' Sean asked, and then he remembered. It had been that day he had been given the black bag by the leprechaun. 'I remember it now.'

The angel closed the book with a thump. 'Well then – that's

108

what you'll do. . .'

It is said that Sean wanders this world still. You can see him sometimes as he roams across the marshes with his lantern. The country people call his spirit, Jack o' the Lantern. . .

The Fairy Harper

In the old times, the fairies would sometimes creep into a house where there was a new-born child and exchange it for one of their own. These children were called changelings, and were often ugly and mischievous. But they usually had a gift – and if you could find that gift, you would be able to use it to send them back to fairy land and bring back the human child. . .

Grania O'Neill stood by the side of the wooden cradle and looked down into it. Her neighbour and friend, Sheila, looked over her shoulder.

'What are you going to call him?' Sheila asked.

Grania tucked the blue blanket in around the tiny baby's chin, and slipped his arms beneath the covers. 'We'll call him Brian, I think,' she said.

Sheila nodded. 'His grandfather is called Brian, isn't he?' She peeped into the cot again. 'Who do you think he looks like?'

Grania shook her head. 'I don't know.' She frowned slightly. 'When he was born I thought he looked like me, and I could have sworn he had reddish hair then.' She ran her fingers through the child's mop of dark hair. 'I must have been mistaken though.'

Sheila glanced down into the cot again and frowned. 'His hair is black,' she said. 'Are you sure it was red when he was born – it wasn't just the light?'

Grania shook her head. 'No, I remember thinking that his hair was the same colour as mine...' She paused. 'You don't think anything's wrong?' she asked.

Her neighbour quickly shook her head. 'No... no, of course not.'

The tiny baby whimpered in his sleep and turned over.

As the years passed, it became very clear that young Brian O'Neill was different from his two brothers and father. They were big and broad and all three had heads of bright red hair. Brian was thin and spindly and his hair was black.

By the time he was five years old, he was a difficult boy, always trying to cause trouble between his brothers, breaking things, telling lies, throwing stones at the dogs and cats. Grania tried to control her son, but it wasn't easy, and her husband, Mark, was out most of the day, tending to the farm with his two older sons.

Now one day, just before Brian's sixth birthday, an old blind harper came to the village. He was called Turlough Carolan – and he was the finest harper in all Ireland, if not the world.

News of the harper's arrival travelled quickly through the village. Carolan was a very famous man, and welcomed everywhere he went, for wherever he went there was sure to be a party.

Sheila came running up to the O'Neill household, 'The harper's come,' she shouted, 'and there's to be a dance tonight in the field beyond the village.'

'Which harper?' Grania asked, 'surely not Turlough Carolan?'

Sheila nodded. 'Yes, Carolan the Harper. Now will you come tonight?' she asked. 'I'll be there.'

Grania nodded. 'I would love to...' and then she paused, 'but what about Brian?'

'Bring him with you,' Sheila said, 'it's probably the only time the harper will come through our village.'

Grania nodded. 'We'll be there,' she said.

So, shortly after tea that day, Grania dressed Brian in clean clothes, while her husband and two older sons also dressed themselves in their best clothes, and then the family headed off into the village towards the field.

By the time they reached the village it was deserted, but

in the distance they could hear a low murmuring and, every now and again, the faint sound of harp.

When they reached the field they found that everyone from the village and nearby houses and cottages had come to hear the legendary harper. Some of the shop-keepers had set up wooden tables and there were baskets of fruit and freshly baked bread for sale, and some people even had huge pots of tea brewing. It was like a giant picnic.

Grania took Brian by the hand and made her way through the crowd to the far end of the field to where an ancient oak tree stood. The tree had once been struck by lightning and had burnt away to a tall twisted stump that looked like a hand closed into a fist, but with the first and little fingers pointing up towards the sky. Between these two pieces of wood there was a sort of natural seat, and the harper was sitting there.

There was quite a crowd around Turlough Carolan. He was a small, stout man, bald and with a pleasant round face that was fringed with tufts of white hair. He was dressed in clothes that had once been fine, but which were now well-worn. There were patches on the elbows and knees and Grania noticed that the sole of one of his shoes had come off, but he was cheerful and seemed to be laughing all the time. His poor clothes didn't seem to bother him.

His hands, Grania noticed, were lovely. They were long and slender, and his little finger was almost as long as his first. His nails were short, but spotlessly clean, and there were hard pads of skin on the tips of all his fingers from the strings of his harp. His harp was also very beautiful. He carried it in a plain soft leather bag, with a simple design running down one side and held closed by two strings. The body of the harp was made of plain black wood, inlaid with a Celtic design in gold, and there were tiny figures of men and animals carved down one side.

When the harper lifted up his harp, the crowd fell silent, and crowded around the small man. He looked up, his blind eyes seeming to look at each one in turn.

'Now, if you'll be so kind as to give me a little room here,' he said in a soft, rich voice.

The crowd shuffled back and Carolan waited until they had moved far enough away. He then took his harp and settled it between his legs and then gently touched the strings. The sound it made was almost silent, and yet it hung on the air like the whistle of a breeze. The crowd sighed – all except Brian.

When he heard the first sounds from the harp, he stiffened and his dark eyes opened wide in astonishment. He squeezed his mother's hand so tightly that she let it go, and then he stood, swaying slightly in time to the music with both hands pressed to his cheeks.

Turlough Carolan played his harp. He played jigs and reels, happy songs, sad songs, old songs and some he had composed himself. He played quickly and then slowly, softly, then loudly. And all the time Brian O'Neill swayed in time to the music. When the harper played fast, the little boy would bounce around and jump up and down; and when the harper played a slow, sad song, the boy even cried.

Some time later the harper took a break. Someone brought him a drink, and he put down his harp and sat back against the ancient tree to rest. The people drifted off into small crowds, laughing and talking together, and no one noticed the small boy creeping towards the harp. He looked up, but Carolan was busy answering questions, with his harp leaning against the tree-stump. Brian reached out and touched the strings with his long, delicate fingers...

The first sounds were like a bugle call. Everyone in the field fell silent and turned towards the sound. Then a series of sharp, clear notes rang out, followed by a quick piece of difficult dance music. Some people began to clap, thinking it was the harper again but Carolan was just as surprised as everyone else.

Grania O'Neill turned when she heard the sounds. She got a fright when she saw her son handling the harp. She was about to reach out and pull him away when the harper's surprisingly strong fingers closed around her sleeve. She turned and looked into his blind eyes.

'Leave the boy,' he whispered, 'let him play.'

Grania looked from him to Brian and then back to the harper. 'How do you know it's a boy?' she asked in amazement.

Carolan smiled. 'A boy plays differently to a girl; he has a different type of touch. When you cannot see, you make your other senses work all the harder. Even though people were talking to me, I heard someone approach my harp. I guessed then that it was a boy, and when I heard him play, I knew.' Carolan smiled quickly again. 'I heard you take a deep breath when you saw who was playing and then I heard you hurrying towards him.' He shrugged his shoulders. 'It's really quite easy.'

Grania shivered. 'It's almost like magic.'

Carolan shook his head. 'No, that's magic,' he said nodding towards the small boy playing the harp. 'Has he been playing long?' he asked.

Grania shook her head, and then, realising that the harper couldn't see, she said, 'No, no, this is the first time he has ever touched a harp.'

Turlough Carolan started. He squeezed Grania's arm tightly, 'The first time? He's never touched a harp before?'

'Never,' Grania said.

The harper looked troubled. 'Is there. . . is everything right with the child? Does he look like the rest of your family?' he asked at last.

'No,' Grania whispered, and then she told Carolan about her son. When she was finished the harper remained silent for a while, but then he smiled sadly, and said, 'Well, we will have to see what we can do now, won't we?'

'I don't know what you mean,' Grania said.

'Don't you worry about it,' Carolan said. 'Let's just listen to the boy play for a while.'

And while Grania and Carolan had been talking, Brian had been playing the harp. His fingers danced across the strings, touching, stroking, brushing, pulling, plucking each one perfectly, as if he had been playing the harp all his life. He played tune after tune, some fast, some slow, some that people knew, and others that were wild and strange.

And when he played these tunes everyone felt their feet begin to tingle and then begin to tap, and they felt as if they had to dance. When Brian saw this, he began to play more and more of this wild, breezy music, and soon everyone was whirling about the field, dancing, dancing, dancing – even if they didn't want to!

Brian laughed then. 'Dance, dance, dance,' he called. He played fast and everyone fairly flew about the field in a dizzy circle, and then he played slow music, and everyone was forced to shuffle. But nobody could stop.

Then Carolan stretched out his hand, and said something in the old Irish language. Immediately the music stopped –

and so did the dancers, frozen into position. Brian touched the strings again and again, but no sound came from them. He looked over at the old harper. 'What have you done?' he demanded.

Carolan smiled. 'My harp obeys me – and only me.'

Brian plucked the strings again, but they hung slack like pieces of wool. 'Make it play!' he shouted.

Then the harper held out both hands and said something in the old language again. The harp seemed to tremble in Brian's hands, and then it began to shake, and suddenly it flew from his grip like a bird and landed safely in the harper's hands. Carolan stroked the strings, whispering gently to it, like a pet.

'Give it to me,' Brian shouted. He stood up and ran towards the old man. But Carolan just smiled and touched the strings, sending out a thin, shivery sound that stopped the boy suddenly He tilted his head up and looked from side to side, as if he was listening.

116

And then Carolan played. His music now was sad and strange, almost lost. The dancers – who were still frozen, though they were able to see and hear – felt the hairs on the backs of their necks begin to itch. They felt a cold wind that smelt faintly of roses and mint touch their skin and most of them suddenly felt very frightened.

They all knew that there was magic in the air.

The harper's music grew wilder. Clouds began to scuttle across the sky, hiding the moon and the stars which were beginning to shine, and it seemed to grow very dark, very quickly.

Suddenly there was the sound of many hooves, as if a troop of horses was approaching. The music quickened and it began to sound like people speaking.

A shape moved through the frozen people, looking like a tall, thin man on horseback. It moved between the harper and Brain, and then, suddenly, it was gone in a clatter of hooves – and so was the boy.

But in his place was a young human girl – with a head of bright red hair...

Afterwards people said that the harper's music was so beautiful that the fairy folk had been forced to come to its call. But some said that Carolan had learned to play from the Sidhe, and that he was very friendly with them, and that they brought the girl back because he has asked them.

Grania and Mark O'Neill called the young girl Nora. She was the baby that had been changed shortly after she had been born. She grew up to be a wise woman, a mná allthacha, and she could do all sorts of cures. But she never liked the sound of a harp – isn't that strange?

The Floating Island

There are supposed to be islands off the west coast of Ireland which float. These are fairy, magical islands, which rise up out of the sea once in every seven years. . .

Louisa loved to walk on the beach late in the evening when the sun was sinking down beneath the waves. She loved the colours of the sunset, the reds of the sea, the pinks of the sky and the blues, greens and purples of the clouds. And every sunset was different. The young girl would sit on the stony beach, with her chin resting on her knees and her arms wrapped around her legs, and watch the sun sink slowly into the wild western ocean.

Autumn was the best time for sunsets. In summer the sun rarely went down until far too late in the evening, and the sunsets then were not really brilliant, and in winter the weather was often bad and sometimes she didn't see the sun all day. But autumn was a really special time.

Louisa was nine years old, and she lived on Ireland's wild western coast, quite close to the huge, black Cliffs of Moher with her mother, father, older brothers and grandfather. She could look out of her bedroom window onto the Atlantic Ocean, and she would sometimes lie in bed and watch the birds flying past her window, coming in from the sea, and she often wondered whether they had flown all the way from America without a stop.

One evening in late September, she was walking on the beach waiting for the sun to set. It was already low over the sea. The sky had changed from a deep blue to a light, hazy purple colour, and some of the clouds were tinged with pink. Louisa climbed up onto a large, flat stone and settled back against it. The stone was still warm from the day's heat, and she closed her eyes and rested her head against the smooth rock. She was a tall, thin girl, with long, thick, black hair that fell to her back. Her face was round and her nose slightly turned up. Her eyes were the colour of grass.

She opened her eyes and looked up into the darkening sky. Far, far above her head, a long V-shape of birds flew slowly across the sky, little more than black dots in the distance. She turned back towards the sinking sun... and then she sat up suddenly. There was something out in the sea.

Louisa stood up on the flat stone and shaded her green eyes. 'What is it?' she wondered aloud.

She could see a long low shape in the water, not big enough to be a ship and too long to be a fishing boat, and Louisa didn't think it was a whale. She stopped and shook her head, squeezing her eyes shut and then looking again. The shape was coming closer.

'What is it?' she asked again. She climbed down off the rock and hurried down the beach, the round stones rattling and clinking under her bare feet. Soon she was standing in the shallow water, her face screwed up tight and her hands shading her eyes from the glare of the sun. The shape was closer now...

'It's an island!' she said in astonishment. But there was no island off the coast here. The next stretch of land after the Cliffs of Moher was the east coast of America, over a thousand miles away. Even as she watched little lights began to glow on the island, and then she found that they helped her to make out the shape. There was an old-fashioned type of house on the island – and, yes, she was right, the island was floating!

And it was coming closer.

Suddenly the sun disappeared beneath the horizon. She had been so intent on watching the strange shape that she had missed the sunset, but now, with the sun no longer blinding her eyes, she found she could see the island and the building quite clearly. The building was a long, low square shape with a low, sloping roof. It seemed to be made out of flat stones set one on top of the other, with huge stones at the bottom and smaller stones set on top. Louisa remembered her father building a wall the same way only a few weeks ago, and he had told her then that it was one of the oldest and safest ways of building a strong wall. He had also told her that some of the most ancient buildings had been made that way.

The stones of the building were wet and dripping and there were strands of seaweed hanging from the higher stones. There was a low wall, which had been made the same way, running around one part of the floating island, and a few small bushes and a couple of ragged, spindly trees, which were also dripping seaweed. The island had a rough stony beach, and Louisa could see a few silver fish flapping on the stones, where they must have been trapped when the island had risen from the sea.

Louisa knew then that it was a fairy island. She had often heard her grandfather tell about the islands of Tír na nÓg and Hy-Brasil which were supposed to lie off the west coast of Ireland, drifting about in a fog bank. She remembered the old man telling her about the other islands which were part of the *Tír faoi Thuinn*, The Land Beneath the Waves, which sometimes rose up from the bottom of the sea and drifted about for a little while before sinking back to the sea-bed again. This must be one of those, she decided.

She wondered if any of the fairy folk actually lived on the island. She knew that there were people in the sea, Mer-Folk and Seal-Folk, and Sea-Horses and Sea-Cows, but did people actually live on the island beneath the waves? She looked closely at the island again.

'I wonder who lit the lamps?' she asked aloud.

'I did.'

Louisa jumped. She turned around quickly, but there was no one there – she was the only one on the beach. She turned back to the island.

'Who are you?' she asked, and then she said, 'Where are you?'

The door in the building on the island opened, throwing a long beam of yellow light out across the water. A tall, thin figure stepped into the light and raised its arm in a wave.

'I am the Woman of the Isle,' the figure said, and then Louisa realised that the woman had not actually spoken aloud. The girl had heard her inside her head. 'I will not harm you,' the woman said.

Louisa hugged herself tightly. It suddenly seemed to have turned very cold. 'What is your name?' she asked.

The Woman of the Isle stepped out of the light and walked slowly down the thin white path that led to the beach. Louisa saw that she was very pale indeed, although both her skin and hair had a slightly greenish colour. She was wearing a gown that looked like it was made up out of long strands of different-coloured seaweed, and she had a simple coral crown on her head. She stopped on the beach, close to the edge of the water, and the island had now drifted so close that there was very little distance between the girl on the

shore and the woman on the island.

'I have no name,' she said at last, and although she didn't move her lips, Louisa heard her quite clearly. She saw her frown. 'No, that is not true; I had a name once, but it was a long, long time ago, and it has been so long since I used it that I must admit that I've forgotten what my name was. What is yours?' she asked.

Louisa hesitated. Names were supposed to have a little magic in them, and if she told this strange woman her name, would she then have power over her?

'I will not harm you,' the Woman of the Isle said slowly inside Louisa's head.

The girl nodded to herself. 'My name is Louisa,' she said.

The Woman of the Isle frowned. 'Louisa... Louisa... Louisa,' she repeated slowly. 'What a strange, beautiful name,' she said. 'I have never heard it before.'

'Surely you can remember your own name?' Louisa asked quietly.

The woman shook her head. 'It has been so long... so long.' She pressed her pale hands to her head and thought hard. At last she looked up. 'It might have been Rhian,' she said.

'Rhian,' Louisa said, pronouncing the strange word slowly. 'Rhian, It's a very lovely name.'

The woman smiled. 'It is a very ancient name.'

'Are you very old too?' the girl asked.

Rhian smiled a little. 'Very old,' she said.

The island bumped against the shore with a crunch of sand and stones, and then stopped. Rhian reached out her hand. 'Would you like to see my island?' she asked.

Louisa hesitated for a few moments. It was getting late and she knew she should be home... but then she decided that if she only went over for a few moments, no one would know. Louisa reached out her hand and hopped up onto the rocky beach of the island.

Rhian, the Woman of the Isle, showed her over the small island. She showed her the bare trees that only flowered once in every hundred years and only bore fruit once in every thousand years – but if you managed to eat some of that fruit you would become immortal – you would live forever. She showed her bushes whose leaves could be woven into the finest cloth, and there was a sort of grass on the island that could be cut and shaped into warm, fleecy blankets.

And then she showed the girl her house.

From the outside it looked like nothing more than a rough stone building with a thick wooden door, but from the inside it was far, far different. Louisa walked through the door and stopped in amazement. Instead of the stone walls and ceiling and bare ground that she expected, she found that she was looking at a beautifully decorated, brightly lit room, with rich tapestries hanging down along the walls, and a lovely thick carpet on the floor. At one end of the room, a huge fire crackled in the grate, and there were two old-fashioned low stools with rounded seats on either side of it.

'But... from the outside,' she began.

Rhian smiled. 'It's magic,' was all she would say. 'Would you like something to eat or drink?' the Woman of the Isle then asked.

'No, no.' Louisa shook her head. Her grandfather had told her never to eat or drink any of the food of fairy land. He had told her stories about boys and girls who had done so and had then been trapped there for years because of it. 'I must go now,' she said, 'it's getting very late.'

Rhian bowed and stood back, allowing Louisa to hurry outside onto the island. Night had fallen and the stars were hard and sharp in the purple-black sky.

'Well, I'd better be getting home,' she said, 'my parents will be wondering what has happened to me.'

'Of course,' the Woman of the Isle said. She raised her long-fingered hand and touched Louisa's shoulder. 'Before you go... is there anything you would like to say to me?' There was a strange look in her eyes as she asked, and her voice sounded strained.

'I don't understand,' Louisa said. 'Except, of course, thank you, you have been very kind.'

Rhian smiled sadly. 'Is there nothing else?'

Louisa backed away towards the beach. 'Well... thank you again.'

'Is there nothing more you can say to me?' Rhian asked, and her eyes were damp with tears.

The girl began to get a little frightened now. She shook her head. 'I've already said thank you,' she said. 'What more can I say?' And then she jumped from the floating island onto the beach. She turned and ran up the beach to the foot of the tall, dark cliffs, the stones rattling under her feet.

And when she looked back the island was gone.

Louisa hurried up the path to her house. There was a light burning in the window and the front door was open. She could see the shape of her father standing in the door, with her grandfather behind him.

'Where have you been?' her father demanded. 'Do you know what time it is? We've been worried sick.'

'I'm sorry,' she panted. 'But wait until I tell you what happened...'

Louisa told her story to her father, mother, brothers and grandfather as they sat around the kitchen table drinking hot tea. Her brothers laughed and thought it was all a great joke, but neither her parents nor grandfather said anything, and in the end her mother sent her brothers to bed because they would not behave themselves. When they had gone, her grandfather asked, 'And did this lady ask you anything as you left the island?'

Louisa looked at him strangely. 'Yes, how do you know?'

Her grandfather shook his head. 'Tell me what you said first.'

'I thanked her for her kindness,' she said.

'And that's all?'

The girl nodded and yawned. 'That's all. Why?' she asked.

Her grandfather smiled a sad little smile. 'That woman was your grandmother,' he said. 'I first met her over sixty years ago, on a night such as this. I didn't realise then that she was of the fairy folk and I fell in love with her. I stayed with her for three nights and when the time came for me to leave she asked me that question. Like you, I just thanked her. What I didn't know was that if I had said *God Bless You*, the island would have remained stuck to the shore and she could have come onto the beach.' He smiled sadly again. 'She appears once in every seven years, looking for someone to say those three words, so that she will be able to come looking for me...'

'I didn't know, grandfather,' Louisa said sadly.

The old man smiled. 'Of course not. And sure, she'll be back in seven years' time. I might meet her then...'

But the floating isle still appears off the west coast of Erin, and the Woman of the Isle is still waiting for someone to say those three simple words, 'God Bless You'.

More Mercier Books

IRISH ANIMAL TALES
Michael Scott

Have you ever noticed how cats and dogs sometimes sit up and look at something that is not there? Have you ever seen a dog barking at nothing? And have you ever wondered why? Perhaps it is because the animal can see the fairy folk coming and going all the time, while humans can only see the Little People at certain times ...

A collection to entrance readers, both young and old.

IRISH HERO TALES
Michael Scott

When we think of heroes we think of brave knights on horse-back, wearing armour and carrying spears and swords. They do battle with demons and dragons, evil knights and magicians. But there are other kinds of heroes: heroes we never hear about ...

Michael Scott's exciting tales capture all the magic and mystery of Irish stories and he brings Ireland's dim and distant past to life in his fascinating collection of Irish hero tales.

STRANGE IRISH TALES
FOR CHILDREN
Edmund Lenihan

Strange Irish Tales for Children is a collection of four hilarious stories, by seanchaí Edmund Lenihan, which will entertain and amuse children of all ages.

IRISH STORIES
FOR CHILDREN
Selected by Tom Mullins

Reading stories helps us all to see life in different ways. We can leave behind our ordinary everyday life and enter into other worlds; these can be real or imagined; we can have adventures with heroes and heroines, with ghosts and giants, with animals and monsters which leave us wishing and wondering.

The stories in this book, selected by Tom Mullins, are from some of Ireland's finest writers and they will delight and entertain children of all ages.

THE CHILDREN'S BOOK OF
IRISH FOLKTALES
Kevin Danaher

These tales are filled with the mystery and adventure of a land of lonely country roads and isolated farms, humble cottages and lordly castles, rolling fields and tractless bogs. They tell of giants and ghosts, of queer happenings and wondrous deeds, of fairies and witches and of fools and kings.

IRISH FAIRY STORIES
for Children
Edmund Leamy

In these stories we read all about the exciting adventures of Irish children in fairyland. We meet the fairy minstrel, giants, leprechauns, fairy queens and wonderful talking animals in Tir na nÓg.

IRISH FOLK STORIES
for Children
T. Crofton Croker

A selection of well-loved tales, including 'The Giant's Stairs',
'The Legend of Bottle-Hill', 'Rent Day' and 'Fior Usga'.

The Children's book of
IRISH FAIRY TALES
Patricia Dunn

The five exciting stories in this book tell of the mythical,
enchanted origins of Irish landmarks when the countryside
was peopled with good fairies, wicked witches, gallant
heroes and beautiful princesses.

Did you know that there are bright, shimmering lakes in
Killarney concealing submerged castles, mountain peaks in
Wexford created by magic, a dancing bush in Cork bearing
life-saving berries, the remains of a witch in a Kerry field and
deer with silver and golden horns around Lough Gartan in
Donegal?

These stories tell of extraordinary happenings long, long
ago and show that evidence of these exciting events can still
be seen today if you only take the time to look carefully.

ENCHANTED IRISH TALES
Patricia Lynch

Enchanted Irish Tales tells of ancient heroes and heroines,
fantastic deeds of bravery, magical kingdoms, weird and
wonderful animals ... This new illustrated edition of classical
folktales, retold by Patricia Lynch with all the imagination
and warmth for which she is renowned, rekindles the age-
old legends of Ireland, as exciting today as they were when
first told.